"Was this supposed to be a joke?"

Elden halted two feet from Millie. "What? What are you talking about?"

"Why did you bid on my dessert? It was to make fun of me, wasn't it? A joke between you and… your friends?"

Elden stared at her blankly. "Millie, I have no idea what you're talking about." He pushed his hands deep into his pockets. "I bid on your dessert because I—" He swallowed, seeming to struggle to get the words out. "Because I wanted to. Because I wanted to sit with you."

"You wanted to sit with *me*?" Millie asked suspiciously.

He nodded. "And have some of that. It looks delicious. It was the prettiest dessert on the tables. Everyone said so." He pointed at the galette Millie was still holding against her chest as if it could somehow protect her feelings.

She bit down on her lower lip, studying his face. He looked sincere and maybe a little scared. Had he *really* paid thirty whole dollars because she had made it? Because he liked her?

Emma Miller lives quietly in her old farmhouse in rural Delaware. Fortunate enough to have been born into a family of strong faith, she grew up on a dairy farm, surrounded by loving parents, siblings, grandparents, aunts, uncles and cousins. Emma was educated in local schools and once taught in an Amish schoolhouse. When she's not caring for her large family, reading and writing are her favorite pastimes.

Books by Emma Miller

Love Inspired

Seven Amish Sisters

Her Surprise Christmas Courtship

The Amish Spinster's Courtship
The Christmas Courtship
A Summer Amish Courtship
An Amish Holiday Courtship
Courting His Amish Wife
Their Secret Courtship

The Amish Matchmaker

A Match for Addy
A Husband for Mari
A Beau for Katie
A Love for Leah
A Groom for Ruby
A Man for Honor

Visit the Author Profile page at LoveInspired.com for more titles.

Her Surprise
Christmas Courtship

Emma Miller

LOVE INSPIRED
INSPIRATIONAL ROMANCE

LOVE INSPIRED®
INSPIRATIONAL ROMANCE

Recycling programs
for this product may
not exist in your area.

ISBN-13: 978-1-335-58603-2

Her Surprise Christmas Courtship

Copyright © 2022 by Emma Miller

For questions and comments about the quality of this book, please contact us at CustomerService@Harlequin.com.

Love Inspired
22 Adelaide St. West, 41st Floor
Toronto, Ontario M5H 4E3, Canada
www.LoveInspired.com

Printed in U.S.A.

Cast not away therefore your confidence,
which hath great recompence of reward.
—*Hebrews* 10:35

Chapter One

Honeycomb, Delaware

"**P**enny is feeling so much better since the visit from the vet," Millie said as she used a pitchfork to toss fresh straw into the goat's stall. It had been her twin sister's turn to clean the stalls, but Willa wasn't much for outdoor chores. Willa thought the barn smelled and she was afraid of mice, so Millie was doing it for her. Millie wasn't scared of anything she could think of. Certainly not a little mouse.

"You remember John Hartman, don't you?" Millie murmured as she pushed the straw around on the packed dirt floor. "From Seven Poplars? He grew up Mennonite but went Amish to marry the widow Hannah Yoder?"

Her mother's favorite goat was getting on in years and Millie wanted to be sure it was comfortable. Past the age of bearing young or even providing milk, the goat had been put to pasture. And Millie figured that having provided for the family for so many years, Penny deserved as good a care as anyone on the farm.

"I'm glad Penny is on the mend. Aren't you, *Mam*?"

Her mother didn't respond.

Tearing up, Millie leaned on the pitchfork. Of course her mother didn't say anything.

Her mother was gone.

The Lord had taken her home more than a year ago.

Unlike her father, Millie never forgot that *Mam* had passed, but she still liked to talk to her sometimes. It comforted her. And maybe she *was* listening. Who knew?

Satisfied that the area was clean, Millie rested the pitchfork against the wall and walked out into the freshly swept aisle that ran between the stalls of the barn. "Come on with you." She took Penny by her leather collar and tugged, but the goat didn't budge. Penny was too busy eating her oats from a bucket. "Going to be stubborn this morning, are you?" Millie asked patiently.

The brown-and-white Nubian bleated and stuck her head back into the bucket.

Millie laughed. "Fine." She stroked Penny's warm, soft back. "You've nothing but scraps left, but you can take them with you." Leading the goat with one hand and enticing her with the bucket with the other, she returned Penny to her stall and closed the door.

According to her sister Henrietta—whom they called Henry—Penny's stall was the last of the three that needed to be mucked. Because her parents had been cursed—or blessed, depending on the situation—with seven daughters and no sons, Millie and her sisters had always done barn chores at their father's side. Now that their *dat* wasn't dependable when it came to such matters, the girls worked on a rotating schedule, with Henry overseeing them.

With the task done, now all Millie had to do was dump the wheelbarrow of dirty bedding and she could return to the house to see if there were any apple pancakes left over from breakfast. The manual labor had made her hungry again. And maybe she'd have a hot chocolate, too. As she hung the pitchfork on the wall, she wondered if there were any marshmallows left. She'd bought two big bags at Byler's store, but her father loved marshmallows and often sneaked them from the pantry. If Millie's eldest sister, Eleanor, found out he was eating handfuls of marshmallows, she'd be cross with him because, according to his doctor, he was supposed to be watching the amount of sugar he ate.

Millie adjusted the blue wool scarf she wore over her head and tied under her chin, and grabbed the wheelbarrow handles. There were a lot of things she didn't like about being a big girl—as her father called her—but one of the good things was that she was strong. As strong as any man. Stronger than some. She could easily roll a whole wheelbarrow to the manure pile without a problem. Whereas Willa, a thin wisp of a girl, had to make two trips.

As Millie rolled the wheelbarrow out of the double doors into the barnyard, she raised her face to catch a few warm rays of the sun. It was early October, and they had woken to the welcome relief of a cool breeze. It had been a long, hot summer and she was thankful for the change of seasons. Plus, fall brought all kinds of delicious foods to the table: sweet yams, apple turnovers and savory cabbage stews. And then there was Christmas to look forward to.

As Millie pushed the wheelbarrow toward the manure pile, she spotted Willa under the clothesline in the backyard. Millie had dressed for barn work in an ugly, stained brown dress and her father's oldest denim barn coat. Willa, however, was dressed for chores in a new peach-colored dress and knit sweater that was more suited for Sunday visiting than house-work. Covering her blond hair, Willa wore a white organza prayer *kapp* rather than a sensible headscarf like Millie.

As Willa clipped a pillowcase to the line, she leaned forward, looking at something in the distance, her pretty face in a scowl. Suddenly she drew back, her eyes going wide, and, spotting Millie, began to wave her arms, shouting something at her. However, between the sound of the howling wind and the creaking of their metal windmill as it spun, Millie couldn't hear her sister. Then their flock of sheep caught sight of her and must have thought she intended to feed them, because they all came running to the fence, bleating and hitting their front hooves on the rails.

Millie let go of the wheelbarrow handles. "What?" she hollered to Willa, cupping her hand to her ear.

Willa began jumping up and down, pointing. It sounded like she was hollering "Wow!" or maybe "Pal!" *Pals?*

"I can't hear you!" Millie called.

Willa ran toward her, flapping her arms. "The wows are out!"

The wows? Millie thought. What on earth was her sister talking about? She turned in the direction Willa was pointing. Then she saw them. Beyond the barn, through several small, fenced corrals and across the pasture was their herd of a dozen cows.

On the far side of the fence.

Millie brought her hands to her cheeks. *The cows had broken out of their pasture!* "The cows are out!" she cried to her sister.

"I know!" Willa shouted, running toward her. "That's what I was trying to tell you! We have to get Henry! She'll know what to do!"

Millie rolled her eyes as Willa came to a halt beside the wheelbarrow. "We don't need Henry. They're our cows, too. Come on," she said, hurrying toward the gate. It would be quicker to cut across the field to the cows than to go around the barn and down their long lane to the road.

"Millie, we can't herd cows," Willa fretted, following her. "That's Henry's job. You know how she is. Henry's not going to like it."

Millie flipped the latch on the gate. "*Ach,* but Henry's not here, is she?"

"She's not?"

"Nay." Millie started across the pasture. "She took *Dat* visiting. Remember?"

"Wait! You're going too fast. Wait for me," Willa called, closing the gate behind her.

"We have to get them before one of them gets hurt," Millie said, refusing to slow down. If Willa weighed half what Millie weighed, she ought to be able to go twice as fast, shouldn't she?

"Oh! Oh my," Willa cried as they crossed the field.

Millie looked over her shoulder to see her sister hopping in one direction and then another, as if moving from one lily pad to another on their pond. "What are you doing?" she asked.

"Cow pies."

Millie had to cover her mouth to keep from laughing aloud. She loved her sister. Adored her. But Willa was what their mother had called *fussy.* Their mother had always said Willa was too persnickety for a farm girl. She didn't like to get dirty or sweaty or touch anything she thought was icky—which was a lot of things.

"I could go back to the house and tell Eleanor the cows are out. She could send Jane or Beth to help you." Willa backtracked, to dart around a patch of high grass.

Millie slowed from a trot to a fast walk, keeping an eye on the cows on the far side of the fence. They were moving along the road, sampling the fresh, uncut grass. She tried not to think about what could happen if one of the cows ventured into the road. The year before, a family in a neighboring church district had lost their only milk cow when it broke through their fence and was hit by a big truck.

Reaching the fence that ran along the road, Millie halted, looking one direction and then the other. Where was the hole in the fence? She'd assumed their two dairy Holsteins and the beef cows had broken through an opening along the road. She had intended to go through the break in the fence and herd the cows back in the way they'd gone out, but there was no break there.

Willa stopped beside Millie, panting. Petunia, the older of their milk cows, lifted her head, chewing a mouthful of clover while she stared at them as if wondering how they had gotten inside the pasture.

"Where did they go through?" Willa asked.

"I don't know." Millie looked in the direction of their driveway to the north, squinting in the hope of seeing the break, but she didn't.

Just then, Petunia began moving toward the road.

"*Nay*," Millie murmured, snatching a handful of green grass and waving it at the cow. "Come this way. Look what I have. It looks so good. Mmm," she said, trying to entice Petunia.

The cow lifted her head but didn't move toward the bouquet of grass Millie held out.

"We have to climb over the fence," Millie told her sister, afraid to look away from Petunia for fear she would take off for the road.

"Climb the fence?" Willa protested. "I'm not climbing a fence. This is my new dress. We'll have to walk back to the gate."

Millie watched the black-and-white Holstein out of the corner of her eye, while continuing to look for the break in the stockade fence. Her father had built it twenty years ago from heavy-gauge wire fencing strung between posts and lengths of lumber across the top of each section. Still seeing no break in the fence, she glanced at the herd again. The other cows seemed content, at least for the moment, to eat along the far side of the fence, but Petunia kept turning away from Millie to look at a patch of thick clover across the road in their neighbor's ditch.

"I'm cold. I should go back to the house and get help." Willa hugged herself for warmth. "Or...or maybe we could get Elden to help." She pointed in the direction of the Yoder farm across the street.

They'd grown up with Elden Yoder and attended school together. He had been a year ahead of them and the best-looking, most popular boy in their one-room schoolhouse. Millie had always liked him; in fact, she liked him so much that she avoided him whenever possible. Even as an adult she felt tongue-tied around him. He'd become engaged earlier in the year, but the wedding had been called off. It had been a bit of a scandal because no one in the town of Honeycomb knew why the betrothal had ended, but there was a lot of speculation. Willa and their youngest sister, Jane, had talked about nothing else for weeks after it happened.

"I don't need Elden Yoder's help to catch my own cows," Millie argued. She looked the stockade fence up and down. "I guess we're going to have to go over it." She dropped the grass she'd been trying to tempt the milk cow with and placed her foot gingerly in one of the squares of the metal fence, testing to be sure it would hold her weight.

"But Elden's right there," Willa said.

"He's right *where*?"

Petunia turned away from Millie and started for the road just as a pickup truck whizzed by.

"Nay!" Millie cried, scrambling up the fence. At the top, she pressed both hands on the board and awkwardly threw her leg over. If she could just hoist herself over—

Millie didn't know what happened next. Maybe her sneaker slipped, or maybe the old wire fencing broke, but suddenly she was falling. It seemed like such a long way down. She cried out as she went over, spooking the cows, who all took off in opposite directions, bellowing and mooing loudly.

"Millie!" Willa screamed.

Millie hit the ground, arms flailing, and rolled down the slight incline, coming to a rest with her face planted in the drainage ditch.

"Oh!" her sister cried from the other side of the fence.

Millie wondered if she had blacked out for a moment because the next thing she knew, someone was leaning over her. And then a deep, masculine voice asked, "Mildred? Mildred, are you okay?"

* * *

Elden had spotted the twin Koffman sisters hurrying across their pasture and had wondered what they were up to. He'd lowered the blade of his scythe to the ground to rest his aching shoulders as he watched. He'd been working on clearing his meadow since breakfast and was thankful for the respite. Then he saw that their cows were on the wrong side of their fence and had dropped the scythe to run to their aid. He was crossing the road when Mildred, head down, not seeing him, had started to climb the fence.

Elden had shouted for her to wait, that he was coming, but he guessed she hadn't heard him in the wind. He was halfway across the road when Mildred tumbled head-over-teacup, as his mother liked to say. And then the girl hit the ground. Hard.

Elden had sprinted the last few feet.

He now crouched beside her as she lay face-down in the ditch, not moving, and he feared she'd been severely injured. He hesitated, not sure if it was okay to touch her, but then gingerly laid his hand on the small of her back.

"Oh my!" Mildred's twin, Willa, fussed from the other side of the fence. "She's broken her neck, hasn't she? She's dead."

"She's not dead," he told Willa. With his hand on Mildred's back, he could feel her breathing. He leaned down, bringing his face close to hers. "Mildred, can you hear me?"

"Millie," Mildred said softly, still not moving.

Elden leaned closer. "What's that?"

Mildred moved her head ever so slightly and opened the eye he could see. He had always thought she had pretty eyes—they were big, and the color of nutmeg with little flecks of cinnamon.

"Millie," she repeated. "No one calls me Mildred. Not since my school days."

Elden couldn't resist a smile of relief. If she was correcting him, she had to be okay, didn't she?

He and Mildred—*Millie*—Koffman had never been friends, even though their families had lived across the street from each other since they were kids. But he had always liked her. Over the years, he'd heard derogatory remarks from others about her being chubby. Some even called her fat, but he had always thought she was pretty. The way he figured, God had made them all in His image and everyone was beautiful in their own way. Millie had beautiful eyes, beautiful golden hair and a beautiful personality. And most importantly, she was a woman of deep faith. Even though they weren't exactly friends, he often saw her at social events. She was always optimistic, never gossiping like her twin, and she had a way of looking at the world that made those around her more positive. "Are you okay, Millie?"

"Fine," she mumbled. "You can go. I'm fine."

He glanced up at the cows that had scattered when she had fallen. Thankfully, none of them had bolted across the road. "You don't seem fine. Can you…can you move?" he asked, worrying that she had broken something when she hit the ground. Why else would she still be lying there?

"I can," she said.

"Then why aren't you? Do you…do you need a hand to get up?"

She looked up at him with her one visible eye. "I'm not moving because I'm too embarrassed."

Again, he smiled. Lots of people got embarrassed, but few ever admitted it. Certainly not to others.

"I'm thinking that if I lie here and pray harder than I've ever prayed in my life," Millie told him, "maybe I'll just die and my mother will come for me."

It was all he could do not to laugh. But he knew better than to do so because then she'd be even more embarrassed. "What? You're embarrassed because you fell going over a fence?" He snorted. "That's nothing. Last Sunday at church, I was carrying a bench, tripped and landed at our bishop's feet in front of the whole congregation."

Millie rolled over onto her side and looked up at him, smiling. There were bits of dead grass and leaves stuck to her face. "It's too bad we're not in the same church district. I'd like to have seen that."

"It was quite a sight, I'm sure." Elden stood and offered his hand to her. "You think you can stand now?"

"Sure." She gazed up at him, her cheeks rosy, the scarf tied over her hair askew. "Just got the wind knocked out of me. You didn't have to come over. My sister and I can round up our cows."

He still held his hand out to her. "If it was my cows loose, would you help me?"

She scrunched up her nose, which made him want to smile again. Goodness, she was pretty. And there was a sparkle in her eyes that made him feel good. Better than he had in months.

"Of course I would help," she told him.

"Then get up, Millie, and let's get these cows back in the pasture." He thrust his hand out to her again and this time, she grabbed it. And when she did, he felt a spark leap from her hand to his. The kind he had feared he would never feel again.

Chapter Two

The next morning, Millie's sixteen-year-old sister, Jane, stood frowning in their bedroom doorway, one hand on her hip. "Eleanor sent me up to see what's taking you so long." She walked in and plopped down on Millie's bed.

"Sorry," Millie, still in her flannel night-gown, said as she gathered clean underclothes from a chest of drawers.

"Eleanor isn't going to be happy if break-fast is late getting on the table," Jane said. "Then dinner will be late." She rocked her head left then right. "Which means supper will be late and she'll be in a bad mood all day fretting over it. You know she likes us to stay on schedule."

Millie sighed but made no comment on their eldest sister's constant need to mother them.

With six younger sisters in the house, she supposed it was to be expected that after their *mam* died, Eleanor, as the eldest, felt she was responsible for taking her place. But Eleanor took the role too far. She fussed over the family more than their mother ever had.

"I didn't mean to lie abed so late." Millie glanced at the battery-powered alarm clock on the nightstand between her and Willa's beds. It was 7:15 already. "I couldn't sleep last night. I don't think I really fell asleep until after three."

Millie didn't tell her little sister that what had kept her awake was reliving over and over again her tumble over the fence. She'd obsessed about the accident that had landed her in the ditch and finding Elden Yoder looking down at her. She'd been beyond embarrassed. She'd been mortified. She'd hoped he'd just walk away and leave her there, but he hadn't. Instead, he'd helped her up and assisted her in finding the break in the fence. Then, after Willa had gone back to the house to report on the situation, he'd helped Millie herd the cows back to the barn.

Millie had gone over in her mind that part of her encounter with him repeatedly, too. His smile. The twinkle in his blue-gray eyes. The jut of his square chin when he'd smiled and the span of his broad shoulders as he walked away.

Somewhere between the ditch she landed in and the barn where he'd helped her give the cows hay, Millie had fallen in love with Elden. She had known at that moment that she'd never love another man. Not that she thought anything would ever come of it. She knew very well it wouldn't. Handsome, kind, hardworking men who owned their own two-hundred-acre farm didn't fall for fat girls like her. They fell in love with and married skinny girls like Willa. In fact, she was certain Elden was already in love with Willa. Why else would he have asked her where Willa had gone after she returned to the house?

"Well?" Jane asked, bringing Millie back to the moment. She gestured with both hands. "Are you coming or not?"

"I'm coming. I didn't expect anyone to wait breakfast on me." Millie went to the corner where her dresses hung on a pegboard on the wall and took down her blue dress. It was her Friday dress, one that made her feel good every time she wore it. And today was going to be an extra good day. She could feel it in her bones.

"*Ach*. Eleanor said to tell you not to wear that," Jane said.

"But it's Friday." Millie clutched the dress to her chest. "I always wear the blue on Friday."

Jane pursed her lips. She was a pretty girl with hair redder than blond that peeked from beneath her starched, white prayer *kapp*. Their *mam* had called the color strawberry blond and hers had been the same shade. Eleanor and Henry had it, too. "Eleanor says it's too short on you and she's expecting a visit from Aunt Judy today. Judy sees you in it, you know she'll go right home to her husband and tell him the Koffman girls are running wild with their short skirts."

Millie wrinkled her nose, thinking about her mother's older sister. "Would Judy do that? I wouldn't think that would be one of the duties of a bishop's wife—tattling on the congregation."

Jane shrugged and got up to start making Millie's bed for her. Willa's and Jane's were already neatly made. "I'm just telling you what Eleanor said. Wear the new beige one she made for you. It's plenty long enough."

"It's long enough, all right," Millie said. "It's so long I'll trip on the hem. You'd think she was making it for herself, it's so long." Eleanor was the tallest of the sisters, taller than their father. She had an imposing way about her and her height made her even more so. "And one sleeve is longer than the other. I wish she'd leave the sewing to Willa. Willa's much better at it."

Jane tucked the handmade log cabin quilt neatly at the end of the bed and began to fluff Millie's pillow. "I'm only telling you what Eleanor said. And she's already in a bad mood because Willa went out to get eggs from the henhouse and only came back with two."

Millie's mouth puckered in indecision as she held up the blue dress with its neat tailoring, looking at it and then the beige one hanging on the pegboard, then back at the blue. She liked the blue one. It went well with her eyes and her blond hair, but she was particularly fond of it because she and her mother had cut and stitched it together. Maybe the blue *was* a little shorter than her other dresses, but it covered her knees and the neckline and sleeves were modest enough to satisfy any bishop in Honeycomb. Especially one new to the roost. Bishop Cyrus had only just been elected to the position in early summer.

Millie made a face. "Why did she only bring back two eggs?"

Jane popped up off the bed. "Because it's Willa," she said as if that was enough. "Whoever heard of an Amish girl who's afraid of chickens?"

Millie headed out the bedroom door on her way to the upstairs washroom, the blue dress still in her arms. "Tell Ellie I'll be right down."

"You better not call her that this morning," Jane called after Millie. "She's not in the mood!"

Ten minutes later, Millie was dressed and ready for the day, whatever it might bring. As she came down the steep steps of their farmhouse, she heard the comforting sounds of mornings with a big family and it made her smile.

Lately, she'd begun worrying about whether she'd ever marry. With so many pretty sisters, so many pretty, thin, unmarried girls in their community, it was only logical that she would be last in line to ever have a beau.

If she was ever actually in line.

But hearing Beth's laughter and the chatter of her sisters, smelling the fresh scrapple and bacon cooking, she decided that maybe it wouldn't be such a bad thing not to marry. If she didn't marry, she could stay home and take care of their *dat*, freeing her sisters, including Eleanor, to marry.

Eleanor had it in her head that no one would

ever marry her because as a baby she'd been diagnosed with a congenital disorder. Before she was old enough to walk, she'd had her leg amputated below the knee and now wore a prosthetic. She moved as fast as any of the sisters—certainly faster than Willa on her best day. And no one would even know Eleanor had a prosthetic leg unless she told them. She was as graceful as the ballet dancers Millie had once seen on Dover's Green at a festival. Eleanor wore regular shoes and the prosthetic looked no different than her other leg beneath the skirt of her dress. But that was Eleanor. She was stubborn the way their mother had been, and once she decided something, she stuck to it, even when all evidence suggested she was wrong.

"*Goot* morning," Millie greeted everyone in the kitchen.

"Cold," *Dat* told Millie, setting down his coffee mug as she walked into the room. He was seated at the head of the long trestle table in their country kitchen. "Don't like my coffee cold."

Millie took a piece of scrapple from a serving platter on the counter, and Eleanor, who was frying bacon, swatted at her with the pair of tongs she was using to flip the bacon.

"You're late," her eldest sister said. "Of

course, I don't know what we're having for breakfast now because we've only two eggs to feed the eight of us."

"Two eggs?" Millie asked, savoring the crispy scrapple. Some folks didn't like scrapple because it was made from the scraps left over after butchering a pig. Plus cornmeal and spices. But she thought those people were just plain silly. God made the scraps the same as He made the pork chops, didn't He? What made one piece of a pig good and another bad?

"We have some leftover potatoes from last night," Cora suggested from her seat at the table where she was reading a book. She was a year older than Millie and Willa and was always reading. Unless she was writing. She was the smallest of the sisters, just five feet tall and wore wire-frame spectacles, which seemed like such a stereotype to Millie—that the big reader in the family wore glasses. She was the only one of them besides their *dat* who had prescription glasses. Their *mam* had never been able to decide if the books had caused Cora's poor eyesight, or if it was poor eyesight that made people readers.

"Is there something wrong with the hens?" Millie asked, not directing her question to anyone in particular.

"Who drinks coffee cold?" their father grumbled. He shook his head in displeasure and tried to pull a page of the *Budget* newspaper out from under Henry, who had a doorknob in pieces on it. "How's a person supposed to read with stuff all over their paper?" he grumbled.

"There's your paper, *Dat*. You already read this one cover to cover." Henry pointed to the latest edition of the nationwide newspaper, still rolled up in front of him. Amish and Mennonite households all over the world received the *Budget* every week. For many, especially the Amish who didn't have phones in their homes, it was a way to keep up with other Amish communities, and family and friends who lived far away. "I'm using an old one to keep the table clean."

Still nibbling on the scrapple, Millie glanced down at Henry's pile of doorknob parts. "He take it off the door again?" One of their father's odd new habits was to try to fix things that weren't broken, often rendering them so afterward.

"*Ya*. Said it was squeaking. Only now there's a part missing. I'll probably have to run to the hardware store."

"Can I go with you?" Cora asked. "And stop

at Spence's Bazaar on the way home. I need more writing paper."

"You need paper or you just want to flirt with JJ Byler?" Jane teased. As she spoke, she set a plate down in front of Cora. JJ's family owned a deli at the bargain flea market and auction that featured Amish food shops, and if he wasn't working construction, he helped out on Fridays and Saturdays.

"JJ Byler?" Cora scowled. "Not interested." She cut her eyes at Willa, who was standing in the doorway between the kitchen and the mudroom, the egg basket in the crook of her arm. "Willa's the one who's sweet on JJ."

"Am not!" Willa argued, but it was only half-hearted, because everyone in the kitchen knew she liked him. Willa had had her eye on him since he'd stopped seeing another girl.

"Well, I hope everyone is fine with scrapple, bacon and toast," Eleanor announced. "Because apparently we're not having eggs this morning."

Millie looked to Willa and mouthed, "Why didn't you get the eggs?"

"Because those chickens are mean," Willa whispered. "They bite."

"Oh, they do not—"

"What does a man have to do to get a hot

cup of coffee around here?" their father bellowed. Which was unusual for him because he rarely raised his voice. At least he hadn't before the dementia had taken hold.

"*Dat*," Eleanor said gently, walking over to him. "It's orange juice, not coffee. Remember? You asked for orange juice this morning."

"It's in a coffee cup," he argued.

"Yes, *Dat*, but look. It's orange juice." She pointed into his mug. "You asked for it in your mug."

"I like my coffee hot," he answered, pushing his round wire-frame glasses up on his nose.

Millie glanced at Eleanor. "I'll take care of *Dat*'s coffee and the eggs." She cut her eyes at Willa.

Eleanor went back to the stove and began to take the bacon from the cast-iron frying pan to lay it on paper towels to drain. "You can't do everything for her all the time, Millie. She's got to learn how to do these things for herself. How's she going to collect eggs at her own house once she's married if she doesn't learn now?"

Millie scooped up her father's coffee mug of orange juice. "That is cold, isn't it, *Dat*?" Then to Eleanor she whispered, "Sometimes I think when he complains it's just that he wants

to feel like he has control over something."
She picked up the old percolator coffeepot that
was being kept warm on the back of the eight-
burner propane stove, and gestured as if to
pour coffee into the mug. Only of course she
didn't. "Hot coffee freshened right up, *Dat*!"

"Who took my old apron, the one with the
hole in the pocket?" Beth demanded, walking
into the kitchen.

Cora looked up from her book to point at
Jane while Jane pointed at her. "She did," they
said in unison. It was a family joke, always
blaming someone else for borrowing each other's things.

"Here you go, *Dat*," Millie set the coffee
mug of orange juice in front of her father.

He picked it up, took a loud slurp and said,
"Now, that's what I call a cup of coffee."

Millie smiled and brushed her hand across
his shoulders. He'd always been a big man,
not tall but muscular, but he was beginning
to look thinner. Some of the hardiness she as-
sociated with him had withered. "Willa and I
will get the eggs," she said to the room. "Be
right back."

Eleanor started in again about it being high
time her sisters got serious about their house-
keeping skills, as Henry dropped something

on the floor and got down on her hands and knees to crawl under the table. At the same time, Cora, who was now setting the table, dropped a plate, startling everyone, including Jane's big, fluffy gray cat, who shot out of the kitchen.

It was a normal morning in the Koffman kitchen and it made Millie smile as she linked her arm through her twin's. "Come on. Let's go get the eggs before Eleanor fries one of us up for breakfast."

"But I don't like chickens," Willa whined under her breath.

"You make them nervous. You have to be calm around them if you want them to stay calm," Millie explained at the back door as she looked around for her barn boots. "*Ach.* Where are my boots?" she wondered aloud, scanning the mudroom that clearly needed *retting* up. "Beth! Did you borrow my barn boots again?" she called out. Beth was the only one who wore the same size shoe as Millie. They both had big feet, size ten if the shoe was generous. Of course that didn't always stop another sister from *borrowing* her boots.

"Just put on *Dat*'s," Willa suggested.

"But they're too big."

"We're just going out to the henhouse."

Willa opened the door that led to the open back porch. "Come on, let's go. Otherwise, Eleanor will pick on me all day."

Millie stared at her father's big, ugly rubber boots that were a good two sizes too big for her. Worse, he had used a permanent marker to write a shopping list on the toes of both boots. Even with the mud caked on the left shoe, she could make out the word *Cookies*, spelled with a *K* instead of a *C*.

Millie hesitated.

"Just put on the boots," Willa repeated impatiently, handing her a barn coat. "And this."

"That's *Dat*'s, too." Millie stepped into her father's boots. "I don't see you wearing our *vadder*'s old clothes."

Willa continued to hold out the jacket, saying nothing.

With a sigh, Millie gave in and accepted the jacket. As she slipped her arms into it, she told herself that Willa had a point. What did it matter what she wore outside? No one was going to see her. Aunt Judy wasn't expected until late morning. "You owe me," she told her sister.

"I owe you what?" Willa asked, stepping out onto the porch.

"I don't know. I'll think of something." Millie closed the back door behind her and gazed out at the barnyard. It was a gorgeous fall morning with the smell of freshly cut corn on the air, and the breeze was cool and refreshing.

As they crossed the yard toward the cluster of outbuildings, she tried to walk without tripping, her feet sliding around in her father's boots. "Did Henry say when she could have a look at the fence where the cows broke through? I hate to see them all cooped up in the small pasture."

"I dunno. I heard her and Eleanor talking about it this morning." Willa swung the egg basket on her arm. Henry already had a whole list of things she wanted to do today, and repairing the fence wasn't on it. "Thanks for going to the henhouse with me, *schweschter*. I know you think I'm just being silly, but chickens really do scare me." She shuddered.

Millie smiled, feeling bad for her sister. She couldn't imagine what it was like to be afraid of things. She had never been afraid of anything, not of snakes or bugs or even trying one of Jane's strange recipes. Jane liked to take an ordinary recipe and add "a twist" as she called it, which might mean bacon in apple crumb muffins or bananas in split pea soup. Some of her recipes were better than others.

"You're welcome, Willa," Millie said. "I just

hope that—" She caught movement out of the corner of her eye and came to such an abrupt halt in the middle of the driveway that she almost tripped in her father's enormous boots. There was Elden Yoder, coming right toward them.

And Millie was dressed in a man's barn coat that was dirty and oversize rubber boots with writing all over them.

She glanced at the house. It didn't usually feel like a long walk to the chicken coop from the back porch, but suddenly it seemed like miles. She didn't want Elden to see her dressed like this, but there was no way, even if she ran, she could get inside before he reached them.

"Willa!" he called, waving to them. He had his little bulldog with him. "Millie," he added. As an afterthought, Millie was sure. Because he was a nice young man. He was too polite to ignore her.

"*Guder mariye.* I was just headed up to your house." He pointed in that direction of the two-story clapboard farmhouse. "Wanted to let you know I patched the hole in the fence. A bit of wire had rusted and the top rail had rotted. The cows must have just pushed their way through. Good as new now. You can let them back out into the pasture."

"*Danki*, Elden." Willa smiled prettily.

Willa had a peachy complexion, unlike Millie's, which tended toward red and blotchy, especially when she was nervous or embarrassed. Like now.

Millie could feel her face growing warm. Elden was so handsome, though he looked as if he could have used a few pounds on him. That morning he was wearing denim pants, work boots, leather suspenders and what appeared to be a brand-new work shirt that was a charcoal color, a shade that made his blue eyes look even grayer. Like any Amish man, he wore a wide-brimmed straw hat with a leather band, but there was a tiny blue jay feather tucked into the band. For some reason, the whimsical feather tickled Millie. Maybe because it was very unlike an Amish man. A feather in a hat wasn't against the *Ordnung* their Old Order community followed, but it was unusual.

As Millie tried to think of something to say, Willa, thankfully, kept talking. Willa was like that. She could talk to anyone, even *Englishers*, and always seemed to know what to say. She never got tongue-tied like Millie did.

"We'll tell Henry," Willa continued. "I imagine she'll be relieved. She was fussing this morning about having too many things to do today. And something about not having something she needed to stretch something?" She looked up at him quizzically.

"Right. A fence stretcher. It's a metal bar used to tighten the metal fencing to make it taut. I brought mine along. Made the whole job go easier. And faster." He looked at Millie. "So... you feeling okay today? After your tumble?"

"You mean my dive over the fence?"

The moment the words came out of Millie's mouth, she wished she could catch them and stuff them into the pocket of her father's coat. Her father's coat that she now realized smelled of cow dung.

Why, oh why, hadn't she taken the extra minute to find her own coat? Millie fretted. Elden must think she looked ridiculous. And the huge rubber barn boots with the writing on them? There was no way he could miss them. But men weren't always that observant. Maybe—

"Going grocery shopping later, Millie?" Elden asked, interrupting her thoughts.

"What?" she asked in an exhalation of breath.

He pointed at her feet, the corner of his mouth turning up in a grin. "Your grocery list."

Millie closed her eyes for a moment. She

was beyond embarrassed now. Beyond mortified. Again. What word was there to describe beyond mortified? "I... My..." She didn't know what to say.

"They're our *dat*'s boots," Willa explained. "We were headed out to the henhouse to gather eggs. Millie is helping me because the hens are mean to me." She held out her finger. "Look. The red one with the speckled wings bit me when I tried to get the egg out from under her."

"Daisy," Millie muttered.

Willa looked quizzically at her sister. "What?"

"Daisy." Millie stared at the gravel driveway between her and Elden. "The hen with the speckled wings, she's Daisy."

Elden laughed, his voice a rich tenor. "You name your chickens?"

Again Millie was embarrassed. It wasn't a very Amish thing to do, to name your chickens. "I know. Our aunt doesn't approve." She held up a finger, imitating her aunt Judy with a high-pitched voice. "And God said, 'Let us make man in our image, after our likeness. And let them have dominion over the fish of the sea, and over the fowl of the air, and over the cattle, and over all the earth, and over every creeping thing that creepeth upon the earth.'"

"I know that verse but not word for word," Elden said. "You have a good memory."

Millie lifted her gaze to meet his and she felt an unfamiliar surge of warmth tickle her empty tummy and radiate outward. It felt something like embarrassment, but different. It also felt exciting. He was looking at her in a way that few people outside her family did. Folks tended to avoid eye contact with big girls like her. But not Elden. At this moment he seemed to…to *see* her.

"I do have a good memory," Millie admitted. "Our *mam* used to say it was a handy thing, except when she didn't want me to remember something she'd said or done that she shouldn't have. Or if she'd tried to hide the cookies. I always remembered her hiding places."

Again, he smiled. "I gave two of our chickens names. My *mam* refuses to call them by their names, though. She's like your aunt. She doesn't like the idea of naming animals. Says God didn't intend us to give them names. Same with the dog." He indicated the bulldog that had dropped to a seated position patiently at his master's feet. "His name is Samson but *Mam* refuses to call him that. She just calls him Dog."

Millie dared a half smile. "Like Willa said,

these are my *dat*'s boots. He wrote on them, not me."

Elden pushed back his hat and laughed. "I didn't think they were yours. They look a little big. But then I thought—" he shrugged "—maybe they are hers. Maybe Millie is a girl who likes plenty of room in her barn boots."

Millie found herself chuckling with him.

"The boots are my fault," Willa piped up. "I made her put them on. Eleanor wanted to make fried eggs to go with our breakfast this morning and I didn't bring in the eggs," she explained. Then she looked at Millie. "We should get the eggs, *schweschter*, before someone comes looking for us."

"*Ya*. And I should go, too," Elden said. "I started clearing the meadow along the road." He gestured toward his property. "I've got a lot of work ahead of me. Hoping to plant it next spring. That's why I was out there yesterday when your cows got out."

It seemed like he was stalling, not ready to go yet. Millie glanced at her sister, whose cheeks were turning pink in the morning coolness. It was no wonder he didn't want to go. Who wouldn't want to gaze at Willa's beautiful face? Did he want to court her? Was that why he'd fixed their fence? Neighbors did things to help each other, but repairing a neighbor's fence when they could fix it themselves—that was being more than neighborly.

"It was nice of you to fix our fence, Elden," Millie heard herself say. "Would…would you like to come to supper tomorrow night? I know Henry will want to thank you. And Eleanor, too, and our other sisters." Now that Millie had started talking, it seemed like she couldn't stop. "Eleanor so appreciates anything anyone does to help us. You know…now that *Dat* isn't well."

Elden lifted his brows. "Supper, huh?"

"*Ya,*" Millie murmured, now feeling less sure of herself. Maybe it was a silly thing to do, to invite him. "To thank you."

And let you get to know Willa better, she thought. Because it was pretty much a given that Elden was still standing there because of Willa. It wouldn't surprise her if they were betrothed by Epiphany. She knew a man like him would never be interested in a woman like her, but the idea of having Elden sit at their kitchen table, even if he was there for Willa, made her heart flutter. Just sitting across the table from him, looking at his handsome face, would be more than enough for her.

"All right if I bring my *mutter*?"

"*Ya, ya*, of course," Millie stumbled, not quite able to believe that he had accepted. *Was* accepting. She couldn't remember the families ever eating together before. Not even when their *mam* was alive.

"What can we bring?"

"N-nothing," Millie stammered, unable to believe he'd agreed to join them. "Six o'clock."

"We'll be here." He smiled at Millie, then nodded to Willa.

When he turned and walked back down the gravel lane, Millie felt her knees go weak.

Elden Yoder was coming to supper!

Chapter Three

The sun hung low in the sky as Elden walked down his gravel driveway, wearing the denim pants and green shirt his mother had recently stitched for him and his going-to-town suspenders. To ward off the chill, he'd pulled on his new barn coat and a black wool beanie his mother had knitted. In one hand he carried a flashlight for the walk home; in the other, the basket his mother had handed him in their kitchen. There was a refreshing breeze coming out of the west and the air smelled of freshly cut field corn, soybeans and, oddly enough, hope.

He glanced at his mother walking at his side in her long black wool cloak and black bonnet. When he'd told her about the invitation the morning before, he'd half hoped she'd suggest he go to the Koffmans' without her. She'd been talking for weeks, months, about how he ought to start getting out again, going to singings and bonfires and mingling with young folks. She insisted his period of mourning what could have been had passed and it was high time he started seriously looking for a wife. One better suited to him than *her*, meaning the woman he almost married. His mother rarely spoke Mary's name. She hadn't since the day he and his betrothed had talked on his porch and Mary had walked away and he'd never seen her again.

Elden pushed the memories of the heartbreak into the recesses of his mind where they belonged. He was in too good a mood to let them ruin his evening. He was excited about having supper with the Koffman family and pleased to be excited about something. About anything. Since Mary had broken their engagement, he'd had a hard time being enthusiastic about anything. He didn't think he'd been depressed so much as…disheartened. He'd had his whole life planned out with Mary, and then it had been taken from him in a split second. With a single brief and confusing explanation from her, all his hopes and dreams had crumbled and fallen at his feet. Elden had known for months now that it was time to pull himself out of the hole he felt like he was in. However, knowing you needed to do something and being able to do it were entirely different things.

It was Millie who was putting a lightness in his step this evening. He was still shaking his head over it. Over her. He'd known Millie since he was ten, when he and his *mam* and *dat* and big sisters had moved to Honeycomb to be closer to his *vadder*'s brother Gabriel. At first, they had rented property nearby, but a year before his father's death when Elden was thirteen, they'd bought the farm directly across the street from the Koffman family. Being a year older and a boy, Elden and Millie had never really been friends, but he had always admired her from afar. She had been a girl of faith, of smiles and laughter. And at some point, when he had glanced away, she had become a woman with the same virtues.

And now he was having supper with her. With her family, he reminded himself. No need to get too excited; this was merely a thank-you supper. She wasn't interested in him. Millie had only invited him to be polite and to show the family's appreciation for his help with the cows and the fence, which of course wasn't necessary. But when she had invited him, he'd said yes without so much as a second thought. It was the first invitation like this he'd accepted since Mary had walked out of his life.

"Couldn't you make that dog stay home?" Elden's mother asked, pulling Elden from his thoughts. She was glancing over her shoulder, her nose in the air in disapproval.

Elden looked back at the little brown-and-white mixed-breed bulldog trotting behind them. He'd found the dog that spring wandering the road, starving and flea-bitten, and on an impulse, he'd brought him home. "*Nay.* Samson goes everywhere with me. You know that."

His mother frowned disapprovingly. "I suppose you'll expect Felty Koffman to invite it in for supper? Maybe sit in a chair at the dinner table?"

Elden chuckled, swinging the basket with dessert his mother had made. He'd told her there was no need to bring anything, but she'd insisted it would be rude not to. When she said she was making dessert, he'd been concerned. Lavinia Yoder wasn't much of a cook. She never had been and her repertoire of what she could bake that was edible was rather small. He had prayed she wouldn't make anything that was unpalatable, and his prayers had been answered because she'd made her usual, rice cereal bars, which were actually good.

"I doubt Felty will invite Samson to his table, but even if he does, Samson will have the good manners to say no, thank-you," Elden teased, knowing she hated it when he gave human qualities to animals. As a child he'd never been allowed to even read books with talking animals. He remembered vividly when she'd taken the book *Charlotte's Web* away from him and returned it to his teacher with strict instructions that he never ever be allowed to read another such book again. He hadn't checked the book or any like it from the school's little library after that, but he had managed to get friends to do so for him and he'd read *Charlotte's Web* from cover to cover three times in the fourth grade.

Elden pushed a small rock with the toe of his boot, making a mental note that it was time to level out the lane again. "Samson doesn't care to dine with folks. He'll wait on the porch, same as he does whenever we go to Gabriel and Elsie's." His father's brother had become more like a father to Elden after *Dat* had passed, and Gabriel and his wife and their adult children were the only folks Elden had socialized with since Mary left him.

His mother harrumphed loudly. She was a formidable woman, nearly as tall as Elden, and what his father had always called pleasingly plump. Her size and how she carried herself made her intimidating to some. He hoped not to Millie. She didn't seem like a woman who could be easily unsettled, but in their culture where a young, unmarried woman was expected not just to respect her elders, but sometimes submit to them, he wasn't sure.

"I've been thinking on the matter, praying, and I've come to believe it was wise of you to accept this supper invitation," his mother said, changing the subject abruptly. She did that anytime she didn't like the direction of a conversation.

He raised his eyebrows. They were nearing the end of their long driveway and he could see the glimmer of lamplight in the windows of the Koffman farmhouse in the distance. "You do? Just yesterday you thought it was a terrible idea."

She pursed her lips, jutting out her chin. "It was only that I was wondering what kind of meal a gaggle of motherless girls could possibly throw together."

"The youngest is the only Koffman sister you could call a girl," he pointed out.

She eyed him severely. "A girl is a girl until she's wed. Only then is she a woman." She went on without giving him a chance to comment. "I always liked Aggie Koffman, you know. God rest her soul. She had a kind heart. But the truth of the matter is that she let those girls run too free. I've heard some call them wild."

Elden pressed his lips together to keep from laughing out loud. His definition of wild was obviously different than his mother's. Anytime he had ever seen any of the Koffman sisters, whether it was at Byler's store, or in their yard, they were always dressed appropriately Plain, their hair and bodies properly covered. As for wild behavior, none to his knowledge ever drank alcohol or smoked like some of the other young women he knew who were out sowing their oats before they settled into the life of a baptized congregant. The closest to *wild* behavior he'd witnessed came from the nineteen-year-old middle sister, Henry, who wore her father's pants under her dress in the winter. He'd caught a glimpse of a pant leg when she was shoveling snow in their driveway the previous winter. But what sensible woman wouldn't wear pants under their skirts in below-freezing weather?

"How could they possibly know how to prepare a proper meal for guests?" his mother asked. "It wouldn't surprise me a bit if we had lunch meat sandwiches and soda pop."

Elden shrugged. "I like sandwiches and soda pop. Especially if it's root beer," he teased.

She looked at him, narrowing her gaze. "A new wife should come to her husband well schooled in household skills. Food preservation, cleaning, sewing, cooking. If a woman can't cook, how does she ever expect to marry?"

"Who says the Koffman sisters can't cook?" he asked, refusing to be annoyed. He was too happy this evening to allow himself to be pulled into his mother's fretting that could easily be interpreted, by those who didn't know her, as negativity. She didn't mean to be critical of others. It was just the way she thought things through. Elden had learned long ago that getting upset with his mother or, worse, confronting her about things she said, only made matters worse. Mostly for him. "If I remember correctly, you bought one of Jane's rhubarb-strawberry pies at that auction a few months ago and said a finer one you'd never tasted."

She clasped her hands together, drawing herself up. They had reached their mailbox and were waiting for a car to pass before crossing the road. The bulldog stood obediently at Elden's side, watching the car intently.

"A husband can't live on his wife's rhubarb-strawberry pie!" his mother exclaimed.

Elden chuckled. "Good thing I won't be marrying Jane Koffman, then, *ya*?"

"I can't believe you invited Elden Yoder to supper, Millie!" Jane exclaimed excitedly, as she turned chicken over in a frying pan with a pair of tongs. "He is *so* handsome. And so single." She giggled.

Millie smiled to herself and continued to set the table. She placed the eating utensils just the way her mother had taught her: fork to the left of the plate, knife on the right and a spoon beside it. The table looked so nice. Beth had picked some wheat still standing in the west field and placed it in a blue canning jar, making a beautiful arrangement for the center of the table. And the meal was going to be outstanding. Millie was sure of it.

Eleanor had decided on serving fried chicken, smashed potatoes, roasted carrots, cinnamon cranberry applesauce and buttermilk biscuits. The kitchen was filled with the scent of the frying chicken and the first batch of biscuits that had just come out of the oven. It all smelled so delicious that Millie's mouth was watering. But she was nervous. She glanced at the big wall clock over the pie safe to see that it was nearly six. Elden would be there any moment and she was beginning to question if she had made a mistake inviting him. Now that he was about to arrive, she wondered what she had been thinking when she had blurted out the invitation.

The idea that his mother was coming as well was scarier. Lavinia was a woman with many opinions and criticisms and she had no trouble expressing them. Because they attended different church districts, even though they lived across the street, Millie didn't cross paths often with her, but when she did, she always tried to get away from Lavinia as quickly as possible.

"Oh dear, look at the time," Eleanor remarked, grabbing hot mitts off the counter. "I knew this was too soon for visitors. And us barely out of mourning."

"It's going to be fine, Ellie," Beth said, opening a jar of the previous year's applesauce. "Your fried chicken is good. Almost as good as mine."

"*Ya.* I love your fried chicken," Millie piped up, wanting to be encouraging. She understood this was a difficult event for Eleanor. "It's that little bit of cayenne pepper you add. And the buttermilk you soak it in overnight, of course."

Eleanor hadn't been thrilled by the idea of Elden and his mother coming for supper and had fussed about having to go to the grocery store to put a decent meal on the table. Her eldest sister preferred to stick to their routine, and it did not include guests on Saturday nights. In fact, Millie couldn't recall having dinner guests since their mother had passed. Before their mother died, they'd had family, friends and neighbors over for supper more than once a week. Anyone who came to the door near a mealtime was invited in and somehow their mother always found enough food to put on a nice spread. There was always enough to go around and then some—like the fishes and loaves of bread story in the Bible.

Eleanor didn't have the same gift of hostessing that their mother had. She fretted about the quality of the food she served, the dishes she served it on and the cost of the meal that would set their budget off-kilter for the rest of the month. But none of that surprised Millie. It was just how Eleanor was. What *had* surprised Millie was the lack of interest on Willa's part in Elden coming over.

Didn't Willa realize that Jane was right? Elden was the best-looking unmarried man in Honeycomb? More importantly, he'd proved he was the kindest man in Honeycomb the day their cows had gotten loose. Maybe Willa hadn't cared all that much because all the good-looking, eligible men were already interested in her.

Jane was still chattering. "Susie told me—"

"Which Susie?" Willa interrupted. She stood in front of their father in the hallway, combing his hair for him.

Millie noticed that their *dat* had put on clean pants, his good suspenders and a blue shirt that Willa had stitched for him. She was glad he'd smartened himself up for their dinner guests. Like their mother, he'd always been a social person and Millie worried about him. He seemed lonely, even in a houseful of daughters who loved him. What she didn't know was whether his loneliness was born of the loss of his beloved wife of twenty-six years, or the loss of his memory.

"Susie Beiler," Jane said, cutting her eyes at Willa, annoyed that she'd been interrupted. "Susie said that her sister—the one who lives in Hickory Grove—said that Elden's mother was the one who drove a wedge between him and Mary."

Shocked, Millie turned to look at her little sister. She'd heard whispers about Lavinia and how she might have come between her son and the woman he had intended to marry, but she hadn't considered they might be true.

"Susie said," Jane continued, going on faster than before, "that Lavinia thinks no one is good enough for her son, and that included Mary Yost. Susie says her mother said she doubts he'll ever marry. Him being responsible for caring for Lavinia, what with her daughters living so far away."

"I heard Lavinia never liked her because she was from Kentucky," Willa offered, walking her father to his chair at the head of the table. At Eleanor's insistence, Willa had replaced the mauve scarf that had covered her head with a proper organza prayer *kapp*. They were all wearing *kapps*, even Henry. "Sit right here, *Dat*. You're going to lead us in silent prayer, right? Once everyone sits down. You remember how to do it?"

Their father eased into his chair looking a bit confused, but he nodded.

"And no matter what Mary did," Jane said excitedly, "Lavinia wasn't satisfied. Nothing was right, how Mary dressed, what she cooked, how she drove her uncle's buggy. Mary was living with her aunt and uncle in Hickory Grove, you know. And Lavinia was so mean to her that Susie said—"

"Jane," Eleanor interrupted. "Haven't you and I, *and* Willa," she added, eyeing Millie's twin, "talked about this?" She didn't speak unkindly, but her tone was firm. "Gossiping is a terrible habit. *And withal they learn to be idle, wandering about from house to house; and not only idle, but tattlers also and busy-bodies, speaking things which they ought not,*" she quoted from the Bible.

"First Timothy," Beth announced. She had the best memory of any of them.

A knock on the back door startled Millie and she looked from the table, where she'd just set down a basket of paper napkins.

"Oh my," Eleanor said in a breathy exhalation." She wiped her hands on her apron, looking quite nervous now. "They're here." She looked at the clock on the wall. It was one minute after six. "Prompt, aren't they?" She gave a half-hearted chuckle. "Someone call Henry. I think she's still in the cellar working on the shelving. Millie, could you answer the door?"

Millie froze, her eyes wide. *No, no, no, not me. Anyone but me*, she thought. "You want *me* to answer it?" she asked Eleanor, her voice sounding squeaky.

A timer went off and Eleanor grabbed the hot mitts again. "*Ya*, you. What's gotten into you, Millie? You invited the Yoders'. Don't you think it would be nice if you greeted them at the door?"

Millie's mouth was suddenly dry. After Elden had repaired their fence, it had seemed like a good idea to invite him to supper, but now she regretted it. She hadn't thought that she'd have to *speak* to him. She didn't want to speak to him. All she wanted was to sit across the table from him and steal glances at his handsome face when no one was looking.

"I… Willa, you should let them in." Millie whipped around to her twin, who was licking chocolate brownie dough off her finger, having sampled Jane's new recipe for double chocolate chip brownies with caramel sauce on top.

"Me?" Willa asked. "I didn't invite them. You did."

A knock came again at the door. This one louder.

"Millie!" Eleanor begged, pulling the second pan of biscuits out of the oven. She shot Millie a look, pleading with her eyes.

Millie took a deep breath, grabbed Willa's

hand, and dragged her through the kitchen and into the mudroom. Through the parted curtain on the window in the back door, Millie saw Elden trying to peer in and she ducked behind Willa and pushed her toward the door.

"Really?" Willa chastised. Then she opened the door, smiling her pretty smile. "Elden, Lavinia. We're glad you could come. Supper's almost ready."

"Good of you to have us." Elden came in, pulling off his beanie and stuffing it into the pocket of his jacket. He looked past Willa and made eye contact with Millie.

She held her breath, wishing the moment would last forever.

Chapter Four

After everyone greeted their guests, Eleanor announced that supper was ready. That prevented Millie from having to figure out where to stand in the kitchen, what to do with her hands and what to say if Elden tried to make conversation with her. As her sisters began to pull out the ladder-back chairs around the large, oak-hewn kitchen table, Millie scooted into a chair two seats to her father's left. It was a plan she had landed on after fretting for hours over where she ought to sit. She had made that decision based on the assumption that Elden, being the only other male there, would be seated to Felty's right. That chair would put Elden in Millie's view, but they wouldn't be directly across from each other, so it wouldn't be obvious she was admiring him.

However, when Eleanor suggested Elden sit to the right of their *dat*, Lavinia plopped down in Elden's chair, leaving Elden to sit next to Willa.

And directly across from Millie, which immediately sent her heart racing.

After their father led the families in a silent prayer of thanks, everyone began passing the heaping platters around, the sisters all talking at once, like any ordinary Saturday night supper. But it was far from ordinary because Elden was sitting right in front of Millie with only a lazy Susan full of condiments between them. When she'd invited him, she'd had in mind that she'd be able to watch him and listen to him talk. But she hadn't meant for him to sit right in front of her! When she opened her eyes following grace and saw him there, she'd feared she wouldn't be able to eat a thing. But once the food came around, she somehow found her appetite.

She was eating a biscuit, listening to Eleanor tell Lavinia about a new quilting circle being organized, when she realized Elden was looking at her. Looking *right* at her. Millie swallowed hard and patted her napkin to her mouth, fearing the honey from her biscuit was in the corners of her mouth. Why was he looking at her, she wondered, feeling heat spread across her face. And then she wished she'd worn her favorite blue dress, even if it wasn't blue dress day.

Elden made eye contact with her, smiled and took a big bite of his biscuit, which had more honey on it than hers. It dribbled off his biscuit onto his third piece of fried chicken on his plate. She smiled bashfully and looked down, scooping up mashed potatoes with her fork. Why did he keep looking at her? He was seated next to Willa, the prettiest girl at the table, maybe the prettiest in Honeycomb.

"My friend Sara is organizing a quilting circle," Eleanor explained to Lavinia, sounding more at ease now that everyone was enjoying the meal. "You should join us. She had the idea to start making quilts before we're asked to donate for one fundraiser or another. She's just had her first baby and she's realizing how much harder it will be to do her chores with a little one on her hip"

"One baby," Lavinia said, scooping more applesauce onto her plate. "That's nothing. It's the second one that upsets the apple cart. Salt," she said to Elden, pointing to the lazy Susan, without so much as a please.

Elden passed her the salt, catching Millie's eye. Millie could tell by the look on his face that he'd noticed as well that his mother had forgotten to ask nicely, but instead of being embarrassed, he looked amused.

"Will you be joining the quilting circle, Willa?" Lavinia leaned in front of her son. "Willa!" she said louder when Millie's sister didn't reply at once.

Willa had been busy talking to Jane and swung around to look at their guest. "I'm sorry, Lavinia. I didn't hear you. What was that?"

"Quilting!" Lavinia said so loudly that she startled their father. "I said I know you must be an excellent quilter."

Jane giggled. "Willa hates quilting."

Willa wrinkled her pert little nose. "I'm not very good at quilting. Our *mam* always said my hand stitching was too higgledy-piggledy."

Lavinia drew back. "I thought you could sew. The new bishop's wife told me you were an excellent seamstress."

"Aunt Judy?" Jane gave a wave. "She must have meant Willa's better at quilting than she is. Which isn't saying much."

Lavinia looked down her long nose at Jane as if the teenager were a fly on the biscuits, and Jane lowered her gaze to her plate.

"Willa's good with a sewing machine. And flirting with boys," Beth piped up.

Lavinia turned her attention to their father. "Willa's a modest girl, isn't she, Felty?"

"What's that?" He tucked the cloth dish towel Eleanor had draped over his chest more tightly into his shirt collar.

"Your daughter." Lavinia raised her voice again. "Willa. The pretty one. I hear she's quite a seamstress."

"I wouldn't know anything about that." Felty looked to Eleanor. "Where are the brownies? I smell brownies."

"After supper, *Dat*." Eleanor patted his arm.

"I like my brownies before supper. Don't you, *sohn*?" He pointed at Elden.

"I do. I like brownies before supper and then again after supper." Elden looked at Millie again, his mouth turned up ever so slightly in a smile.

She felt herself blush again and looked down at her plate.

"Speaking of fundraisers," Lavinia said, looking past Elden to Willa again. "I suspect you heard about the apple social coming up next Saturday at the Masts' orchard."

Before Willa could respond, Lavinia went on. "Here's how it's going to work. All the single ladies will bring a dessert." She held up one finger. "But no one is to know which dessert belongs to which girl, then the single men will bid on the desserts and have the privilege of sharing with the baker. A pretty girl like you, I know you're going." She smiled at Willa. "You can ride with us."

Willa stared at Lavinia and then cut her eyes at Millie, the look on her face obvious to anyone who knew her. Willa was saying, *Help me*, without the words coming out of her mouth.

"What do you say?" Lavinia pressed, leaning so far in front of her son that her nose was practically in his plate. "Elden can drive us." She smiled again, but this time her smile was different. It was…sly. "And I imagine he'll be able to figure out what you've made because it will be in our buggy." She sounded pleased with herself.

Looking embarrassed, Elden studied a spot on the far wall, and Millie couldn't decide whom she felt worse for, Willa or Elden.

"Shall we pick you up, Willa?" Lavinia asked. "Or do you want to walk over? Not to worry, Felty," she threw over her shoulder. "I'll chaperone."

Everyone at the table had gone quiet except for the girls' father, who was singing an old hymn to himself as he sawed on a biscuit with his knife, cutting it into bite-size pieces.

Eleanor leaned over to speak softly to their father. "Pick the biscuit up with your hand, *Dat*. No need to cut it."

"Well, Willa?" Lavinia asked, her tone changing in pitch.

"I… I…" Willa stumbled.

Then Eleanor came to the rescue. "So nice of you to invite Willa," she said, looking directly at Lavinia. "But we'll be attending as a family. *Dat* will expect her to go with us." Her gaze flicked to Willa and then back to their guest, her smile matching Lavinia's.

To Millie's knowledge, there had been no talk of attending the social. Since their mother's death they hadn't attended anything as a family except church. It had been too hard for them without their mother.

"I'm sure we'll see you there," Eleanor went on diplomatically. "I think it sounds like a nice day. The Masts' orchard is such a pretty place to have a gathering. I understand they'll be closed for business the whole afternoon to host us."

Lavinia sat back in her chair. "I don't see why—"

"Sounds like it's settled," Elden interrupted, finishing the last bite from his plate. "Delicious meal, Eleanor. Thank you. You're every bit as good a hostess as your mother."

Millie looked at her eldest sister and saw tears in her eyes. Eleanor had done a good job with the meal, but the fact that Elden had made a point of saying so made Millie's heart swell. Eleanor deserved the praise, but coming from their neighbor, it would mean so much to her. Elden seemed to have sensed that. There weren't many men who could stop for a moment and consider a woman's feelings.

And Eleanor had handled Lavinia's pushiness quite well, Millie thought. But why didn't Willa want to go with them to the apple social? That would make it almost a date with Elden, and he would make such a good husband to her sister. Millie was going to tell her so just as soon as they had a moment alone. It was time Willa thought about marrying. A man like Elden, living across the street from them? Not only would he make a good husband to her sister, but he would be a good son-in-law for their father, and a good brother-in-law for a gaggle of sisters.

"Just a little something we threw on the table, but *danki*," Eleanor said to Elden, her face reddening with pride. "We'll have to do this again. It's been too long since we had friends in our home." She glanced at their father. "*Dat* likes it, I think."

"You're a blessed man, Felty," Elden said. Then he looked around the table at the sea of white *kapps*. "Now, what's this I heard about freshly baked brownies?"

Millie met the following Saturday with a mixture of excitement and anxiety. Eleanor had been true to her word and the entire family had packed baskets of homemade apple desserts to be auctioned off at the Masts' frolic. They'd also brought sandwiches and fruit in case anyone got hungry. After the auction there would be softball and volleyball games and those who stayed through supper or returned after feeding their animals would be able to enjoy a bonfire. The annual event benefited all three of the Amish schools in Honeycomb and would be an afternoon of eating, playing games, laughter and friendship.

Millie loved social gatherings and was thrilled to be attending one after their long year of mourning. And it felt good to not be so sad. But she was also nervous about a whole handful of things, none of which she had any control over. Would her father have a good day? This was the first time many people in their community would see him at a social event since the death of his wife, and his health had suffered greatly in those long months. Before Millie's mother died, there had been subtle signs that her father was struggling with his memory, but they had hidden it well and only those closest to him had seen it. But then, after he lost his beloved wife, his mind began to slip quicker. He still had good days when it seemed as if the illness had been Millie and her sisters' imagination. But then there were days when he couldn't remember how to use a toothbrush or called Eleanor by their dead mother's name.

Next on Millie's worry list was Willa. Millie wanted so badly for the day to go well for her—for her and Elden because he would certainly bid on her apple crumb cake cookies. Willa just needed to forget about JJ, who courted a different girl every month, and give Elden a chance. Millie imagined Willa and Elden spending time together on a blanket under an apple tree and love blossoming. The thing was, Willa didn't seem all that interested in spending time with Elden. Millie couldn't figure out if Willa was nervous or what, and when she'd asked her, Willa had dodged the subject, not really giving an answer.

Millie also worried who would bid on her salted caramel apple galette. She knew the dessert tasted as delicious as it looked. She'd made it twice that week to practice and barely gotten a sliver of it herself each time before it was inhaled by her family. But would the young man who bid on it be sorely disappointed when he realized whom he would have to spend time with?

It had happened the spring before her mother died. Millie had attended a lunch basket auction in Seven Poplars with her sisters, and Harry Renno had bid on it. Then, when Millie identified the basket as hers, she'd seen the look of disappointment cross his face. He'd ended up inviting all nine of his younger siblings to join them for the picnic and Millie had spent the hour trying to keep the children from falling in the pond while Harry ate. He hadn't been mean to her exactly, but it had still hurt when he admitted he'd thought the basket belonged to the "pretty Koffman girl"—meaning Willa.

"Millie!"

Her friend Annie Lapp tugged on the sleeve of her dress, bringing Millie back to the moment. Millie was wearing her blue dress—even though it wasn't Friday. They were standing in the sun beside the Masts' back porch where they could observe the activity. Buggies were still coming up the driveway and the yard was full of women of all ages in colored dresses and white *kapps*, dropping desserts off. Men, young and old, clustered in groups talking horses and crops and the previous Sunday's sermons. Dozens of children, boys and girls, raced between the adults chasing each other, laughing and enjoying the perfect fall day.

Jim Mast, who owned the orchard, and several of his sons were putting the desserts they would auction off on plastic folding tables they had lined up under a big sugar maple that was shedding its red and oranges leaves, sending them fluttering across the yard. Jim's wife, Edna, was directing the setup and fussing at her son Freeman, who had stuck his finger under plastic wrap to taste a bit of frosting on a cake.

"Did you hear *anything* I just said?" Annie asked indignantly.

"Sorry." Millie smiled sheepishly. She and Annie always stuck together at social events. They'd been friends since they were children and had always gotten along well. They understood each other. Annie was a pretty girl with dark hair and dancing green eyes, and she was big like Millie. In fact, she was bigger. Hanging out together, they had learned, made it sting less when no one asked to drive them home from a frolic.

Annie sucked on a piece of butterscotch candy. She'd offered Millie one from her apron pocket, but Millie had declined. "I said you were right. Look who's talking to your sister."

Annie pointed and Millie followed her line of vision.

Beyond the tables of desserts, she spotted Willa and Elden standing next to each other. Deep in conversation, Willa was smiling up at him, which made Millie smile. Her chest tightened a bit, though, seeing them getting along so well. He would make a good husband for her sister. And it would be so wonderful to have her twin living across the street after she was married. Millie always worried that Willa might meet someone visiting from another state. It happened all the time. If that happened, once Willa was wed, she might move away as far as Wisconsin or Kentucky and they would rarely see each other.

Annie sucked loudly on her candy. "You think Elden's asking her which dessert is hers so he can bid on it? You're not supposed to do that, but boys sometimes do."

"If he's smart, he's asking her." Millie continued to watch them, and while she was happy for her sister, she was sad for herself. Even though she knew it would never happen, she realized she wanted to be the one smiling up at Elden Yoder.

For a split second, Millie imagined spending the afternoon with Elden and him asking if he could court her. She imagined them riding home together from frolics in a courting buggy, maybe even holding hands when no one was watching. She imagined planning a life together with Elden, a life of happiness and joy in a marriage like her parents had shared.

Of course that would never happen. But it was fun to daydream.

"Look at the way she's smiling at him," Annie said, rummaging around in her pocket for more candy.

Millie watched as Willa said something to Elden and he nodded. Then Willa walked away, her *kapp* strings fluttering at the nape of her neck as she said something over her shoulder to him. A moment later, JJ walked over to Elden and the two men put their heads together.

"Oh, dear. What am I going to do if Junior Yoder bids on my apple pear pie?" Annie fretted. "The last time I had to eat with him, he started telling me how he liked a woman with meat on her bones. Right before he took his false teeth out and set them on his knee so he could gum his supper."

Millie pressed her lips together so as not to giggle. Twice Annie's age, Junior was widowed and had had his eye on Annie for months. He owned a huge farm and still had three children at home, and had made no bones about wanting to make Annie his wife. He'd even gone so far as to speak to Annie's father, Jeb, but nothing had come of it because Jeb didn't want his only daughter married to the hog farmer, either.

Just then, Jim Mast rapped one of the plastic tables with a rubber builder's mallet he was using as a gavel. "Just about ready to get started here," he bellowed. Jim was a small man with a ruddy face and a big Adam's apple, always cheerful, always ready to help someone in need in their community. With eleven children, ages three to twenty-five, he was busy sunup to sundown, but the smile on his face seemed glued there.

"Come on closer, men," Jim coaxed. "Don't be shy! We've got plenty of good eats here. You know how it's done. Bid on a dessert that looks tasty to you and enjoy some time with the girl who made it." He held up one finger. "Of course it's supposed to be a secret who made what."

"What if I want to bid on my girl's pie?" his son Jon called.

Jim winked at the gathering crowd of *kapps* and straw hats. "Then you best bid high because I think your brother Freeman has his eye on the same girl."

Everyone burst into laughter, except for Mary John Beiler, who covered her face with her hands in embarrassment. They all knew she and Jon Mast had been walking out together for weeks. And everyone *also* knew that Freeman Mast liked nothing better than to get under his brother's skin.

"Should have brought two pies, Mary!" shouted a boy from Seven Poplars who was known to be courting one of Jim Mast's girls. "Then you could sit with the both of them."

More laughter followed, then the auction began in earnest. Jon did outbid his brother for Mary's pie. And one after another, the rest of the desserts were auctioned off. Millie's sister Cora's apple muffins were bought by Andy Kertz, Annie's cousin, and Beth and her platonic friend Johnny joined them on a blanket with Beth's apple raisin cookies and a big jug of homemade cider the Masts sold in their shop.

Millie watched apprehensively as Jim auctioned dessert after dessert off to husbands, beaus and single men hoping to meet a girl who might become their wife one day. As the event wound down, Millie kept eyeing Willa's cookies, which would, because of the order of the desserts on the tables, be auctioned off ahead of Millie's galette. But then, Jim started grabbing random plates, and the next thing she knew, he was holding up her galette.

"My, my, my," Jim said tipping the square wooden tray Millie had put it on. "Have you seen anything so beautiful?" He leaned down and took a deep, exaggerated sniff. "And the smell of it!" He shook his head in amazement and Millie felt herself blush.

"I wish you could smell this because you're all going to wish you had a slice of it," Jim went on. "In fact, I might just snitch a piece before I turn it over to the man blessed to win the bid." He looked up at the crowd that had dwindled as couples and families had taken their sweets and settled on the grass or in lawn chairs on the edge of the apple orchard. "Let's say we open the bid at five…no, no, this is too fancy a dessert for five. Eight dollars. Eight is the opening bid."

"Eight," a male voice called. "I'll pay eight." The bidder looked in Millie's direction.

It was Ronny, Annie's brother, who was as wide as he was tall. Ronny wouldn't be awful to spend an hour with, though Millie had kept her distance from him since Epiphany. At a holiday gathering at Matt and Ellen Beachy's place, he'd tried to kiss her behind a buggy when they were out of sight of others. When Millie had pushed Ronny away, he'd fallen into the snow so hard that she'd felt bad and given him a hand getting up before telling him that if he ever tried that again, he'd get worse.

"Good start, good start," Jim encouraged. "But come on, boys. You don't bid higher than that, I'll be winning the bid and Edna and I will be digging into it with the person who made this fine dessert."

"Ten dollars," Junior Yoder shouted.

Annie giggled and squeezed Millie's arm.

Millie groaned. *Come on, Ronny*, she thought. *Outbid him. Please outbid him. I'm not in the mood to look at Junior's false teeth for an hour.*

"Twelve dollars!" Ronny shouted, moving closer to the front of the crowd. Then he glanced over his shoulder and made eye contact and Millie realized he knew she had made it. Annie must have told her brother. Millie couldn't decide if she was angry or happy, because the truth of the matter was that at the end of the day, it was nice to be appreciated, even if it was by Ronny Lapp.

"Fourteen," Junior declared with a raise of his hand.

Millie groaned again.

"I've got fourteen," Jim called. "Fourteen is generous, but who out here is feeling even more generous than that? Remember, this is for a good cause. Money goes to all three schools. We've got books to buy and the school over on Clover Road needs a new floor in the coat room after that leak this spring."

Murmurs of agreement rippled through the crowd. The auction *was* for a good cause, and if that meant Millie had to look at Junior's teeth for an hour, she could somehow do it for the benefit of Honeycomb's schoolchildren, couldn't she?

"Last chance, Ronny. You sure you don't want to part with a couple more dollars for this—what did you say it was called, Edna?" Jim asked his wife, his wide forehead crinkling.

"A galette," she told him, rolling her eyes. "How's a man get to be fifty-some years old and not know an apple galette when he sees it?"

Again, there was more laughter from the friends and neighbors, but the warm kind that was obviously meant only in jest.

"Guess I can go sixteen," Junior said kicking at a clump of grass as his feet.

"Sixteen." Jim pointed. "Going...going—"

"Thirty," a male voice shouted.

Everyone's eyes got big and they began to murmur under their breath as they looked around to see who had spoken.

"Thirty?" Jim asked, looking past Millie to someone in the back. "Are you bidding thirty dollars or thirty apples, *sohn*?"

Everyone laughed and the elderly John Mast, Jim's father, gave a hoot from a lawn chair near the tables, slapping his thigh as if it was the funniest thing he had ever heard.

Then came the voice again. "Thirty dollars, Jim. Cash money."

Millie recognized the male voice now, except that she had to be mistaken. It couldn't be...

"Not going to give it to me all in quarters, are you?" Jim shouted back good-naturedly.

As Millie turned to look over her shoulder, she heard Elden say, "Nope. Nice clean, crisp bills, fresh from the bank."

Millie stared at him thinking, *Oh my, he's somehow gotten mixed up.*

Had Willa told Elden about Millie's galette when they were talking? When Willa told him she'd made the cookies, had he somehow gotten confused and thought Millie had made the cookies and Willa had made the galette? At any other moment, that might have made Millie laugh. A galette was beyond Willa's baking skills. Willa had burned two sheets of cookies, then underbaked one and had to make another batch of them that morning. Jane had helped her with the baking this time, which was the only reason Willa had a dessert to donate at all.

"Junior?" Jim asked. "Got another bid in you?"

Junior shook his head.

"Ronny?"

"Nay." Annie's brother scowled, obviously disappointed.

"Good enough," Jim announced. "Then this fine apple—" he looked at his wife "—*galette* goes to Elden Yoder. Congratulations. I'm jealous. I just hope the special girl who made this will be willing to share the recipe with my Edna." He gazed at the cluster of people. "Who's the fine lady who baked this?"

For a moment, Millie just stood there wishing

she could close her eyes and disappear. Or get down on her hands and knees and crawl away.

"Don't be shy. Someone made this dessert," Jim called out.

Annie nudged Millie. "Speak up," she whispered. "Elden Yoder just bought your dessert."

"It's mine," Millie croaked, raising her hand in the air. "I… I baked it," she said loudly.

A woman gasped and harrumphed. Lavinia.

Suddenly feeling as if she couldn't quite catch her breath, Millie searched for Willa in the crowd with her eyes. She was standing with two of her friends near the table with only a few desserts left on.

I'm sorry, Millie mouthed silently.

Her sister knitted her brows questioningly.

Meanwhile, Elden had made his way to the front, handed Edna his cash, which the older woman tucked into a sewing box. The next thing Millie knew, Elden was standing there in front of her, the galette on the wooden platter in his hands.

Annie giggled, squeezed Millie's arm and excused herself with a shy mumble to Elden.

"Where do you want to sit?" Elden asked Millie.

Millie stared at him, not sure what to say. "Did you make a mistake?" she whispered.

"Mistake? What do you mean? *Nay*, I didn't make a mistake. I love an apple…apple…" He seemed to be squinting, though she couldn't be sure, since he was wearing dark Ray-Ban sunglasses. "What's it called again?"

Realizing this had to be some kind of cruel joke, Millie thrust out her jaw. "What? Do you think you're funny, making fun of me?" she demanded. A lump rose in her throat, and she fought the tears she could feel all scratchy behind her eyelids. On impulse, she grabbed the platter from Elden's hands and strode away, leaving him to stand there and watch her go.

Chapter Five

Pushing up on the brim of his straw hat, Elden watched, perplexed, as Millie walked away. *What had just happened?*

Women were so hard to understand.

After the mention of the apple frolic at the Koffmans' the weekend before, he had mulled over the idea of bidding on Millie's dessert so he could spend time with her. Eleanor's dodge of his mother's invitation to Willa had been clever and had left the door open for Elden if he chose to walk through it. But was he ready?

All week he'd vacillated, going between telling himself he wasn't yet fit to court another woman and thinking about Millie. It kept going through his mind how pretty and intelligent she was and how kind she was to her sisters and father. She'd been through such a tragic loss and yet she had found a way to smile, to laugh, and he envied that. He envied her.

Elden eventually landed on the idea that there was nothing wrong with spending an hour or two with Millie at the orchard. It was for a good cause; he had to bid on someone's dessert. Why not Millie's? Getting to know her didn't mean he had to walk out with her. For all he knew, she wasn't interested. Though he had a sneaking suspicion she was because of the way she had looked at him across the supper table Saturday night when she thought he wouldn't notice. Elden's heart still ached over the loss of Mary, but since the incidence with the cows—with Millie—the ache hadn't been so overwhelming. Now his loss felt more like a blister that was still sore but healing at last.

Once Elden decided that he wanted to bid on Millie's dessert, the trick had been to find out what she would bring to the auction. He hadn't been bold enough to ask her directly but had decided to ask Willa once he arrived. When he told Willa what he wanted to know, she had seemed pleased and given up the secret. In return, he'd offered to let JJ, the boy she was sweet on, know what *she* had made. And it had all seemed to be working out; Elden had been thrilled when he'd won Millie's apple galette. He thought she'd be happy that it was him and not Junior or Ronny, but somehow it had gone all wrong. Did Millie dislike him so much that she didn't want to spend a single hour with him?

Elden watched Millie striding away with determination. She was almost to the barnyard and headed straight for her family's wagon. His impulse was to go after her but then he had second thoughts. What if she really didn't want to sit with him in the orchard? After all, Mary had made it clear that not only did she not want to share any desserts with him, but she also didn't want to live in the same state. Was this another rebuke? Should he abandon the idea before he embarrassed himself even further? The town had been gossiping for months about his breakup with Mary. Would this just throw wood on the fire?

As he watched Millie in her pretty blue dress walking away, he knew he had to go after her. He had to try to find out what was wrong.

Elden felt a tap on his shoulder. "What do you think you're doing, *sohn*?"

His mother's voice startled him and he whipped around. "What?"

She threw her hands up in the air. "You bid on the wrong dessert. I *told* you which one was

Willa's. *Ach*, you certainly don't give the impression of a man as smart as I know you are."

Two girls in matching brown dresses walked past them with blatant interest in their conversation.

His mother ignored them. "But don't worry. I can fix this." She glanced over her shoulder toward Jim who was still auctioning desserts. "You're going to have to hurry. Willa's cookies are about to come up. They're in the square basket." She laid her hand on his arm. "*Square basket*," she repeated. "I'll tell Millie that you bid on her apple whatever-it-is for me. So I could visit with her." She beamed at him. "See. All's well that ends well."

He glanced at Millie again. She had stopped before she reached her family's wagon and was now standing in the lane, the plate in her hand, her head hung low. He looked back at his mother. *"Nay."*

She frowned. *"Nay* what?"

"I am *not* bidding on Willa's cookies. I told you that this morning. And yesterday. And the day before. I'm not interested in Willa Koffman."

"A pretty girl like her? Of course you're interested in her. It would be so convenient for you to marry her. Then she'd be right across the street from her poor father. But she's not going to marry you unless you court her and you can't court her if you don't speak with her." She nudged him. "Go bid on her cookies."

"*Mam*, I don't want Willa's cookies," he said, his tone firm. "I want Millie's apple galette. That's why I bid on it."

"Elden Yoder, surely you're not interested in a—"

"Let it go, *Mam*," he interrupted, not sure exactly what she was going to say but sensing he wasn't going to like it. "We've discussed this. I'm not your little boy anymore and you can't keep trying to make decisions for me."

"But Elden!" she cried after him as he walked away. "This is not the plan!"

He kept walking, his gaze fixed on Millie's back.

Millie heard Elden's footsteps in the gravel behind her. Hot tears threatened to spill and she wiped her eyes with her sleeve. She didn't know what to do. Did she throw the fragrant galette in the field and walk home?

"Millie?" Elden called, fast approaching. "Millie, what's wrong?"

Her lower lip trembled. As she saw it, she had two choices. She could run or she could confront him. In a split second, she spun around, hugging the wooden platter to her chest. "Was this supposed to be a joke?" she demanded.

He halted two feet from her, drawing his head back. "What? What are you talking about?"

"Why did you bid on my dessert? Why did you bid all that money? It was to make fun of me, wasn't it? A joke between you and...and JJ? Your friends?"

Elden stared at her blankly. "Millie, I have no idea what you're talking about." He pushed his hands deep into his pockets. "I bid on your dessert because I—" He swallowed, seeming to struggle to get the words out. "Because I wanted to. Because I wanted to sit with you."

"You wanted to sit with *me*?" she asked suspiciously.

He nodded. "And have some of that. It looks delicious. It was the prettiest dessert on the tables. Everyone said so. Like it came from a fancy bakery." He pointed at the galette Millie was still holding against her chest as if it could somehow protect her feelings. "None of us could figure out what that icing was."

She bit down on her lower lip, studying his face. He looked sincere and maybe a little scared. Had he *really* paid thirty whole dollars for some sliced apples arranged on a piecrust because she had made it? Because he liked her? "It's caramel. And bits of salt to bring out the taste of the brown sugar and butter."

"Ah. That's why Willa called it a *salted* apple caramel galette," he said. "I didn't even know what a galette was. Willa had to explain it to me."

She lowered the tray a bit. "You and Willa were talking about my galette?"

"I asked her what you brought so I could bid on it."

Her eyes widened. "You did?" She thought for a moment. "But wait, why didn't you ask *me* what I made?"

"Because…" He hesitated. "I guess I was afraid you wouldn't tell me."

She narrowed her gaze. "And you didn't want Willa's cookies? *Willa*," she added.

"Willa's a nice girl, but—" He hesitated and then went on. "But I wanted to visit with you."

Her gaze flicked in the direction of the auction. Every dessert was gone from the table and the remainder of the crowd had wandered off. She saw Willa and JJ walking, their heads together in private conversation. He was carrying her woven willow basket of cookies.

Millie looked back at Elden, studying his face. He had blue eyes that were so pale they looked gray. She didn't know many folks with gray eyes and she found them intriguing. His eyes were easy to read. And his eyes told her he was telling the truth. As hard as it was for her to believe. "You're sure you want to visit with me?" she asked again, just to be sure she had understood correctly. "Not Willa."

"*Not* Willa," he repeated.

"But your mother wanted you to bid on Willa's dessert. She invited Willa to come with you today. She has her eye on Willa for you to court."

He exhaled, pulling one hand out of his pocket to drag it across his face. "My mother has good intentions, but it's not up to her to say who I—" He halted again, seeming to choose his words carefully. "Whose dessert I choose to buy."

Millie giggled. Maybe she should have been embarrassed that she'd earlier misread his behavior and stomped off, but she wasn't. Now she was just happy, so happy that she was giddy. "I can't believe you paid thirty dollars for three dollars' worth of apples and flour. Are you always this thrifty with money?"

It took him a moment to realize she was

teasing him. And then he began to laugh. "Three dollars? Come on. It must have cost you more than that. What about the caramel?"

"Elden, caramel is just sugar that's browned and then you add some butter and some cream. A little salt thrown in at the end makes it salted caramel." She cocked her head, looking at him. "But then I guess you wouldn't know that, would you? Because you probably don't make a lot of caramel."

"*Nay*, I do not." The tone of their conversation had changed entirely and now it was almost flirtatious. "I love caramel, but I buy it in a jar at Byler's."

"Your mother doesn't make it?"

He lowered his voice conspiratorially as he took a step closer to her. "You know my mother isn't much of a cook. Never learned. Everyone in the county knows. When my sisters married, their mothers-in-law had to teach them both."

Millie balanced the dessert platter with one hand and covered her mouth with the other, giggling behind it. He was right, everyone *did* know Lavinia Yoder was a terrible cook. Folks in Honeycomb were always on watch to see what she brought to a potluck so they could avoid it. Lavinia had once brought a cheesecake pie to a barn raising and no one had touched it, so Millie had taken a slice so that she wouldn't feel bad. It was one of the worst things she had ever put in her mouth, and that included the beetle a boy at school had once dared her to take a bite of. Lavinia's cheesecake pie had somehow curdled, and it had taken two cups of cider for Millie to get the taste out of her mouth after she spit it into a napkin.

Millie lifted her gaze.

Elden smiled at her and her insides melted like the sweet caramel she'd poured all over her galette that morning.

He glanced over his shoulder and tipped his head. "You want to find a place to sit down and let me taste my three dollars' worth of apples that I paid thirty for?"

She pressed her lips together, knowing her cheeks had to be bright red. "*Ya*, I do. I have a blanket in our wagon we can use to sit on the grass. And I brought a knife and plates and a fork."

"Let's get them, then. I'm thinking over there on the edge of the lawn, near that big Red Delicious tree." He pointed at the tree that was laden with shiny apples, then took the galette from her. "Better let me carry that. I spent good money for it."

Millie grinned as she walked beside him toward her family's wagon. She was so happy that her heart was pounding. Elden Yoder had bought her dessert and he wanted to visit with *her*. Then suddenly, she stopped short. "What about your mother?"

He had to pull up fast to keep from running into Millie. "What about her?"

"Should we invite her to join us?" *Say no, say no,* a little voice shouted inside her. *But that wouldn't be charitable, would it?* "There's plenty," she said brightly. "And I brought some sandwiches in case anyone is hungry."

He frowned, looking unsure of himself again. "Do you *want* her to join us?"

Millie didn't know what to say. She was worried this was a test. Maybe she should say yes. Elden's mother was widowed, he was her only son and she was under his care. Perhaps he wanted to see if Millie would be willing to include her in an activity with them. Maybe the rumors were true and Lavinia had run his fiancée off and he knew Millie knew.

But what if it was a test of a different sort? What if he was trying to figure out if Millie liked him? If she said she wanted Lavinia to share the dessert with them, would he think she didn't want to be alone with him?

Elden waited for her reply.

"What do *you* want to do?" she asked haltingly.

He sighed. "I'm going to be in hot water over this for sure, but *nay*. I don't want to invite her. Her gaggle of friends are all together." He indicated a group of older women seated in folding chairs borrowed from one of the church wagons. "She can join them. None of the other single men are sitting with their mothers."

Millie met Elden's gaze, smiling. "*Oll recht*," she whispered, thinking this might be the best day ever.

By the time Eleanor took up the reins and the family's wagon rolled toward home, the sun had set and there was a chill in the air that signaled that fall had, at last, come to Honeycomb to stay. Millie, Willa and Jane sat on the tailgate of the wagon, their legs dangling the way they had when they were children and their mother had still been here with them. Had it been any other day, Millie might have felt sad that her world had changed so drastically in the past year. But she was too happy to let herself be sad for things she couldn't change. *Gott* had His ways and, as her mother had reminded her often, questioning those ways only made a person discontent.

Millie's afternoon with Elden had been like a dream. She still wondered if she ought to pinch herself. After their misunderstanding, he had carried the picnic basket and the galette to the old Red Delicious apple tree. There, he'd spread out the blanket and in front of half of Honeycomb, he sat with her and ate slice after slice of her apple galette. And he'd eaten not one, but two of her egg salad sandwiches and drunk a full Mason jar of apple cider.

Millie had been so nervous when they sat down that she'd barely been able to eat, but as the minutes ticked by, she'd relaxed a bit. She found Elden so easy to talk to that she soon felt as if they had been friends their whole lives, rather than acquaintances. They hadn't talked about anything important. They'd recalled their school days together and covered numerous other topics: her mother's death, his dog, his plans for his east field that he was clearing and the fact that butter pecan was their favorite ice cream. Then, when the little groups had scattered, he'd helped her tuck the basket back in her wagon. There, she'd wrapped up the galette in aluminum foil and given what was left of it to him to take home for breakfast the following day.

Then, still talking, they wandered over to watch the softball game. When Elden's cousin Daniel had insisted he joined their team after their catcher injured his hand on a foul ball, Elden had at first said no. But then Millie had agreed he should play and she'd stood on the sidelines, clapping and cheering when Elden made a play at home plate and got JJ out, winning for his team.

Millie and Elden had later stood in the Masts' backyard talking as a long line of open wagons and black buggies went down the lane headed home for folks to prepare for church or visiting day the next morning. Millie had known it was almost time to go, but it had been such a wonderful day that she hadn't wanted it to end.

Then Lavinia had marched across the lawn toward them. She barely acknowledged Millie when she announced she was tired and wanted to go home. Elden had met Millie's gaze and murmured good-night. Then they were gone and Millie had nothing but the memories. But they were good memories and she would hold them close to her for the rest of her days. Because she knew there were a hundred reasons why it would never happen again.

"Millie? *Hallo*?" Jane waved a hand in front of her face, a hand she couldn't miss, even in the darkness. "Did you hear anything I just said?"

Millie blinked, pulling her wool cloak closer, glad she had brought it. Because while it had been a beautiful day with temperatures rising to the mid-sixties, once the sun had set, the temperature had quickly dropped. "Sorry, Jane."

"I was telling you that Susie said that a bunch of girls were talking about how Elden must be looking for a wife again. They were talking about how he's now Honeycomb's most eligible bachelor and Susie said the girls were going to get their mothers to invite him and his mother to Visiting Sundays. They were making guesses as to who he'd ask out first now that he's gotten a little practice in with you."

"Jane!" Willa said sharply to their little sister sitting between them on the tailgate. "That isn't very nice!"

"What?" Jane looked at Willa. "I'm just telling you what Susie said the girls were—"

"We promised Eleanor no more gossiping, Jane. Remember? You know very well…"

As Willa chastised their little sister, their voices faded and Millie stared at the paved road as they rolled over it. She listened to the comforting sound of their horse's hooves as his metal shoes hit the blacktop, and the sound of their father, slumped between Eleanor and Beth, snoring.

Against her will, tears welled in Millie's eyes and she wiped them away impatiently, hoping her sisters were too busy quarreling with each other to notice. Jane wasn't saying anything Millie didn't already know. Of course, Elden would begin dating again. And when he did, he would choose one of those pretty girls, one of those slender girls.

One his mother would wholly approve.

Chapter Six

Elden's uncle Gabriel, stood beside him, watching as Elden set the new propane hot water heater squarely in the center of the overflow pan. "I appreciate you coming by to help me get this in," Gabriel said. "I probably could have installed it myself, but it would have taken me half the day." He chuckled. "And that broken one would have been a bear to get out of the house on my own. These old bones don't move as well as they once did." He tapped his temple. "I have to remind myself of that sometimes. I'm not the strapping young man I once was."

"I don't know." Elden glanced at him. "You're pretty fit for a man in his mid-sixties."

"Tell that to your aunt. If she had her way, I'd be sitting at her kitchen table all the day long so she could keep an eye on me. The woman gets herself worked up if I lift anything heavier than a carton of eggs."

Elden smiled and pointed to the toolbox he'd brought along. "Could you grab that pipe wrench for me? Top tray." He could hear his mother chattering a mile a minute to his aunt Elsie in the connecting kitchen.

"I don't know what all he was thinking," Elden's mother said, slurping her coffee. "Just trying to be nice, I suppose. But it's high time he put this whole Mary business behind him and started looking seriously for a wife. Neither of us is getting any younger. I want grandbabies before I'm too old to enjoy them. Look at you, Elsie, with nine and two more on the way."

Aunt Elsie said something, but Elden didn't catch it. Aunt Elsie was a soft-spoken woman of few words—the complete opposite of his mother. And Elsie knew how to mind her own business when it came to her adult children, a trait he knew for a fact his cousins appreciated.

"But I suppose I should look at his behavior at the Masts' positively." Another slurp. "You have any more honey, dear? This coffee is bitter. You should buy the kind I buy. I'll write it down." *Slurp.* "Having practically half the county see my Elden showing such an act of charity will only make girls more interested in him."

Elden grunted as he realized he hadn't threaded the water connection on the top of the new heater correctly and unscrewed it to try it again. He pulled the roll of Teflon tape from his pocket and rewrapped the threads. Then, still not at the correct angle, he moved to the other side of the unit, closer to the kitchen.

"You know all the young women of marrying age at the apple frolic were talking about how handsome my Elden is. And how kind," his mother went on, making no attempt to prevent him from hearing her. As if she hadn't already made her opinion obvious. In the two days since the frolic at the Masts' orchard, she'd managed to bring up the subject nearly every time they exchanged words. Which was why he had jumped on the offer to come to his uncle's today rather than later in the week. What Elden hadn't considered was that his mother would insist on coming with him. "Surely you wouldn't keep an old lady from her sister-in-law, one of her dearest friends," his mother had proclaimed loudly in front of Gabriel when he stopped at their place to ask if Elden could help him with the water heater.

"Their parents think he's a good catch as well," his mother continued without seeming to take a breath. "I wouldn't be surprised if I didn't have mothers coming to me to arrange Sunday visits. You know, that's the way we did it in our day, Elsie. Mothers got together and matched their children. This whole idea that a young man knows what woman would make the best wife for him?" She laughed. "Nonsense. Pure nonsense. *Nay*, a mother knows best."

"Here you go. More honey." Elsie's voice.

"Thank you. And maybe another cookie or two? I do love your shortbread. I keep meaning to get the recipe."

As Elden tightened the water connection correctly this time, he heard what sounded like a jar being set down on the kitchen table. His mother always put so much honey in her coffee that it no longer tasted like coffee.

"I don't know, Lavinia," came Elsie's patient voice. "Millie Koffman is an awfully nice girl. She's a hard worker and she's always patient with her father, no matter what he gets into. You understand he's unwell, don't you?"

"A daughter's duty," Lavinia responded, her spoon clunking against the inside of her coffee mug rhythmically as she stirred. "He seemed well enough the night we had supper with him. Except that he likes his biscuits cut in bite-size pieces, but what man doesn't have odd habits, hmm? But I won't argue with you that one of the Koffman girls might be suitable. It would be so convenient. My Elden courting one of them. Willa is the prettiest of the lot and I'm sure she's kind to her father…but maybe Beth would be suitable," she added thoughtfully. "She has a pretty smile. Not as slender as Willa, but we can't all be so thin, can we?"

Elden gritted his teeth and checked the fitting again, verifying it was snug. Next, he tackled the heat trap fittings. As he worked, he noticed his uncle eyeing the open kitchen door.

"My worry is that Elden has given poor Millie the wrong idea," his mother said. "And then we'll have another mess on our—"

Gabriel slid the pocket door closed between the kitchen and the laundry room with a bang. "Women's chatter can give a man indigestion," he joked.

Elden set his jaw. "I think I'm ready for the pressure relief valve now." He put out his hand.

Gabriel walked over to his propane chest freezer, where Elden had laid out all the parts needed to connect the new hot water heater.

"You know your *mutter* means well," he said quietly.

"I know she does."

Gabriel walked back with the valve in his hand, but he didn't pass it to Elden. "That doesn't mean she knows what's best for you."

Elden chewed on that for a moment.

"I can only imagine how hard losing Mary the way you did had to be," Gabriel said. "But I believe *Gott* had a different plan for you."

A moment of silence passed between the two men, but from behind the door, Elden could still hear his mother talking.

Gabriel cleared his throat as if considering whether to say something else and Elden glanced at him. He looked so much like Elden's father that sometimes seeing him brought a lump up in his throat. His uncle was the same height, white-haired with wire-frame glasses and a face wrinkled by sixty-five years of laughter. And some hardships, including the loss of a child, the death of the brother who was his best friend, and Elsie suffering a debilitating illness early in their marriage that had taken her some time to recover from. But like Millie, Gabriel always had a smile on his face and a sparkle of mischief in his eyes. Unless of course he was angry with something or someone, and then, like Millie, he could speak directly.

Remembering how Millie had snatched the galette from him and stomped off, Elden smiled. The girl had fire in her and she was strong-minded. Which wasn't a bad thing. At least a man knew where he stood with a woman like Millie. Which had obviously not been true with Mary. Otherwise maybe they could have talked things out and tried to work on their relationship rather than having it end so abruptly.

"I'm going to just ask you straight out." Gabriel met Elden's gaze. "You like her? The Koffman girl? Millie?"

Afraid the tone of his voice might suggest just how much he liked Millie, Elden only nodded.

Gabriel shrugged. "Then do something about it."

"But what?" Elden reached for the valve, but his uncle pulled it out of his reach.

Gabriel spoke softly so their conversation wouldn't be overheard. "One thing Lavinia is right about is that it's time you moved on. Mary broke your heart. We all know that. But the fact is, like it or not, she's gone, and she's not coming back. Those are the hard facts.

Which means it's time you find someone better suited to you." He hesitated. "Ask Millie out."

Elden grimaced, the idea terrifying. He had given Mary everything he had and it hadn't been enough. Could he ever be enough for Millie? Did he even deserve a fine woman like her? Was he even meant to have a wife? "Like on a date?" he asked.

Gabriel shrugged. "If you're not ready for that, maybe start slow. Invite her for the Visiting Sunday coming up. Invite the whole family. I heard over at the mill that Felty did well at the apple frolic. Seemed more like himself. He might enjoy visiting as much as his girls would. It's time the whole family started getting on with life. It's been more than a year now since Aggie passed. She wouldn't want them to mourn any longer. Young women are meant to be out and about."

"Invite her for Visiting Sunday?" Elden echoed.

Gabriel nodded, stroking his white beard. "And Elsie and I can come, too, if you like. I'll ask Elsie to keep Lavinia busy. Give you and Millie time to talk."

"We don't usually have folks over on Visiting Sundays."

"Nope, you don't. Not since Mary left, at

least. Which means it's high time you started up again. It will be good for your mother, too. Give her someone else to listen to her." Gabriel cracked a smile, still holding the valve just out of Elden's reach. "What do you say?"

"You really think I should invite Millie— all the Koffmans," he corrected, "over on Sunday?"

Gabriel smiled as he passed the valve to his nephew. "I do think you should invite her. Before some other young man catches her fancy. That dessert she made Saturday was the talk around town. Heard it from three different men at church yesterday. All talking about how they wished their wives could make one of those beauties. Ed Swartzentruber said his wife was thinking about getting their son Danny to take Millie home from the harvest frolic coming up. It's going to be a big to-do. I heard the matchmaker from Seven Poplars is bringing some young men from farther afield. You don't want someone from Ohio sweeping Millie off her feet before you've had a chance, do you?"

Elden thought back to the time he'd spent with Millie on Saturday and how good she had made him feel. How good it had felt to enjoy himself like that again. She'd been so much fun and she could talk about anything.

She had seemed interested in most subjects, even boring stuff like what he was planning to sow in his east field once he had it cleared. "*Oll recht.* I think I will invite the Koffmans. I'll go over after we're done here and extend the invitation. Take Samson with me."

"Good idea." Gabriel pointed at his nephew. "But just the dog. Not Lavinia, if I was you."

They both laughed.

Millie was down on her hands and knees, trowel in hand, planting the last of the fall bulbs in the flower beds flanking the front stoop. Her mother had loved the way tulips, daffodils and crocuses popped up after a long winter. She had said that it was one of the comforting signs that spring had returned and with it, new life in *Gott*'s world. Their mother, an avid gardener, had painstakingly dug up every tulip bulb once it had bloomed. She stored them in their cellar, hanging from the rafters, sorted by color and type.

In the fall, their mother replanted them and Millie and her sisters had waited eagerly for spring to see the new beds their *mam* had created. Every year they looked different. Sometimes there were beds of a singular color—scarlet red, bright yellow, white or her favorite black. But she had also mixed colors: black and white, yellow and red.

Millie liked flowers well enough, but she didn't have the passion her mother had for gardening. She did, however, have a passion for keeping her *mam*'s memory alive, so when none of her sisters had the time or desire to fuss with the bulbs, Millie had dug them up. And now it was time to plant them again before they got a hard frost and the ground began to freeze. She knew the flower beds wouldn't look anything like the neat rows and intricate patterns her mother had planted, but she would do her best.

After putting the job off for a week, Millie had decided today was the day. However, she quickly realized it may not have been the best choice because it was also her day to spend time with her father. *Spending time* with him meant keeping him safe and out of trouble so that Eleanor wouldn't wind up giving them both a scolding over something. Millie had thought her father might enjoy helping her and had given him the task of cutting off the dried tops of the bulbs they had hung in bundles in the cellar. She showed him how to cut the tops off with gardening shears and explained that all he had to do was put them back in the same pile he had taken them from. She had patiently explained to him that it was important he do it that way so the colors wouldn't get mixed up. But either her father didn't understand, or he didn't care to do it the way she'd asked.

Millie glanced over her shoulder to watch her father pull a bulb from the red tulip bundle, cut off the top and toss it into the pile of yellow jonquil daffodils. "*Dat*," she said gently. "Put it back in the same bag, right?"

Without looking at her, he took a bulb from the pile of black beauties, topped it and added it to the giant whites. Millie sighed. She couldn't decide if she should give up for the day and wait until tomorrow to plant the bulbs, or push through. After all, her rows of bulbs were so wiggly, was it going to matter if the colors were mixed? They would still be pretty come spring, wouldn't they? And the following day, she and Willa and Beth were planning on going to the Masts' orchard to pick apples and she didn't want to miss the outing.

"*Dat*, would you like to try planting some of *Mam*'s bulbs? I could dig the hole and you could set them in. How does that sound?"

Her father, on the ground on his knees, pulled his handkerchief out of his pocket and wiped his nose. "Not much interested in planting. Aggie wouldn't want me interfering with her flowers. I think we best wait for her."

Millie sighed but didn't remind him that his wife was gone. There was no point, because when he was having this sort of day, when his mind was clouded, he'd only forget and have to be told again and again.

Her *dat* cocked his head. "Hear that?"

"Hear what?"

"A dog. We get a dog?" He glanced around curiously. "Blue died."

How could he remember that they'd lost their bluetick hound that spring, but not that his wife was dead?

"I don't hear a dog, *Dat*."

He stuffed his handkerchief back in his pants pocket as he slowly got to his feet and turned to the lane that led to the road. "That looks like a dog to me."

Then Millie heard a bark. From her knees, she spotted Elden's bulldog. Shading her eyes from the sun, it took a second for her to see that someone was coming up the drive with the dog. It was Elden.

And here she was on the ground again. Her apron was covered in dirt and it had blueberry stains from the jam her father had spilled on her while trying to make his own peanut butter and jam sandwich. And she was wearing the ugliest dress she owned, complete with a torn hem she'd been meaning to repair.

"Afternoon, Felty," Elden called with a wave.

Felty tipped back his straw hat. "Afternoon, neighbor. That your dog?" He pointed at the bulldog trotting at Elden's feet.

"He is. Name's Samson."

"Good name for a pup." Felty whistled between his teeth to beckon the dog, tapping his thigh. "Come here, boy. Come on."

The dog panted, excited, but didn't move from his master's side. He kept looking up at Elden.

Elden raised his hand and the dog took off across the grass toward the older man.

Millie smiled as her father got down on one knee and greeted Samson with a pat and a laugh. "Nice boy. Good boy," Felty said, stroking the dog's back.

"*Dat* likes dogs," she said. She was still on her knees, debating whether or not to get up, because sometimes it was hard for her. Often she would grab onto something to heave herself up. She couldn't decide which would be more embarrassing—staying on the ground or having to haul herself up like a feed sack. "He misses our dog."

Elden nodded and walked over to her, leaving Samson to entertain her *dat*. "Whatcha doin'?"

"Planting my *mam*'s tulip and daffodil bulbs," she said, deciding she wanted to get to her feet. The question was, did she risk trying to do it without any help? To use the railing of the stoop, she'd have to crawl across the grass to get to it. "Trying," she murmured. Then she said a silent prayer, pressed her hands to the tops of her thighs, and was blessedly able to get to her feet without so much as a wobble.

Elden slid his hands into his pockets. He wore work pants and a barn coat, and his blue wool beanie pulled low on his brow. Today he wasn't wearing sunglasses, so she could see his blue-gray eyes.

"You like planting flower bulbs?" Elden asked.

Millie twisted her mouth one way and then the other. "I like seeing our *mam*'s flowers in the spring, so—" She shrugged. "I guess, in a way, I do like planting them."

Elden smiled nostalgically. "Her flowers were always so beautiful. I remember that spring a few years back when both sides of your lane at the road were a mass of red and yellow tulips. Don't know if I ever saw anything so stunning."

His kind words made her eyes scratchy. She didn't know many men who felt that way about flowers. Her father never had. It just wasn't in a man's makeup, she'd always thought.

But maybe she was wrong. At least about this man.

"You want to play?" Felty said.

Millie looked past Elden to see her father on his feet. He had a stick in his hand. "You know how to bring it back to me?" he asked the dog. "I throw it and you go get it and bring it back. Wanna try?"

Elden smiled. "Samson can fetch, all right. If he isn't being lazy," he told her father. He looked back at Millie. "Nice that your *dat*'s helping you. Good for him to get outside, I imagine."

Millie sighed. "*Ya*, he does like getting out of the house and out from under Eleanor's thumb. She fusses over him more than he cares for, but it's hard doing things with *Dat* sometimes. He doesn't understand—" She stopped, worrying she was saying too much. Talking too much.

Elden waited for her to finish her sentence.

Millie didn't know what came over her. Ordinarily she wouldn't share something like this, but she told Elden about the flowers being organized by color and what a mess her father was making of it. As she spoke, she heard her voice getting shaky and was afraid she might start to cry. Because deep down, she realized, she wasn't upset about the flowers but rather the fact that her father couldn't do what she'd asked. And it made no sense because he could still beat any of them at checkers.

If Elden heard frustration or sadness in her voice, it didn't seem to make him uncomfortable. He listened and then said, "Has to be hard, Millie, to watch him change. I saw the same in a great-uncle I had when I was a kid. Before we moved here." He met her gaze with unblinking eyes. "Felty's a blessed man to have a daughter like you. Daughters like you and your sisters."

She wiped at her eyes with the back of her dirty hand. "If you'd seen him throwing a fuss over how Jane had scrambled his eggs this morning, you might not think so."

She smiled tentatively and he smiled back.

"So…so I came by to ask you something." Elden hooked his thumbs in his pockets. "Um, if your family wants to come for Visiting Sunday, this Sunday coming up."

"You want us to come visiting?" she asked,

unable to contain her excitement. "We haven't been visiting much since *Mam* got sick. I used to love Visiting Sundays."

He drew his hand across his mouth, smiling behind it. "We haven't been visiting much, either, nor had much in the way of visitors, not since—"

He went quiet and she knew what he was thinking. He hadn't been participating in the tradition of visiting with family, friends and neighbors on the off weeks when his church district didn't have services since his betrothal had ended. It was the first time he'd brought up the subject of his betrothal to Mary Yost and the breakup, even in a roundabout way.

When Millie realized he wasn't going to say any more, she nodded, touched that he would broach the subject of his betrothal, even if he hadn't been able to say the words. "I'd love to come. *We* would love to come," she corrected, not wanting him to think that she thought it was a date or anything. But wishing it was. "I'll check with Eleanor, but I'm sure we can come."

"Good." He nodded. "I'll tell *Mam*. And… and my uncle and his wife are coming, too. And maybe one of their sons and his family. We'll see."

His hands were back in his pockets and there was a slightly uncomfortable silence. Millie felt like she should say something but didn't know what. Thankfully, her father ended the awkward moment.

"Good dog you got here, *sohn*." Felty, now seeming light on his feet, walked over to Elden, the bulldog at his heels. "Good dogs like this are hard to come by. We had a hound dog, Blue. Best dog I ever had. But he passed. I like to think he's in heaven with my Aggie." He pointed at Elden. "But don't tell my bishop I said that. I don't think he thinks dogs go to heaven."

Elden and Millie both stood there for a moment, staring at her father. That was the most she had heard him say at one time in weeks, maybe months. And he sounded so clear-headed. Almost like the *dat* she had known her whole life. Elden picked up on it, too. She could tell by the look on his face.

Elden glanced back at Millie. "Guess I better keep my eye out, else your *dat* will steal my dog."

They both looked at Samson, who had dropped to the dying grass at her father's feet, his muzzle between his paws.

"Well. Guess I best get on with the rest of

my day," Elden said. "Got to walk out and check my deer stand."

"Be time for hunting soon, won't it?" Millie asked, hating to see him go. He was so nice and so easy to talk to. And he just made her…happy.

Elden worked his jaw. "I'm not much of a hunter. My *mam* would tell you I'm too soft. But my property can only support so many deer. They have to be culled every year so the rest will survive. My cousin hunts on our property and always gives us more venison than the two of us can eat."

"Mmm," Millie's father said, rubbing his belly. "I do love a good venison stew." He held up an arthritic finger to Elden. "But you've got to cook it low and slow in the oven all day to get it tender. That's how my Aggie always did it."

Elden nodded and then looked to Millie again. "So…see you Sunday? If not before."

He threw the last phrase in as if it was a second thought and she wondered what he meant. Was it just something impulsive he said, or was he *hoping* to see her again before Sunday?

Elden tapped his leg to call his dog and Samson came to his feet but didn't move away from Millie's father.

"You leaving already?" the older man asked. "Taking my dog?"

Millie couldn't tell if her father thought Samson was his dog or if he was just teasing.

"Sorry to say I am. I've got to take a walk through my woods." Elden hesitated and then met Millie's eyes and looked back at her father. "If you feel like taking a walk, Felty, you could join me and Samson. Not much more than a mile there and back."

Millie's gaze shifted to her father. She was immediately unsure of what to say. Sometimes her father didn't have the energy to move from one room to the next. Would he be able to walk so far? Would Eleanor want him leaving the property without one of his daughters? And was that too much responsibility to give a neighbor? What if her father became difficult?

"I—I don't know," Millie stammered. "Elden, you don't have to..."

Elden shrugged. "I'm thinking Felty and I and Samson would enjoy a walk together. Beautiful day for it. I don't know how many more we'll get. The woods are gorgeous right now with all the leaves changing. What do you say, Felty?"

Millie's father looked down at Samson. The bulldog looked up at his new friend.

"Think I would like to take a walk." Millie's father suddenly seemed to stand taller. "Just you and me, right?" he asked Elden.

"Just you and me," Elden repeated.

Her father nodded thoughtfully. "Be nice to get away from these women for a few minutes. Sometimes a man just needs some time away from skirts and bonnets."

Elden tried to suppress a smile as he met Millie's gaze and she pressed her lips together to keep from giggling. *Danki*, she mouthed.

He broke into a wide grin. *Gern gschehne*, he mouthed back.

Chapter Seven

Sunday, just before one o'clock, Millie walked halfway down the porch steps, then turned and ran back up. In her rush to get out the door, she had forgotten the basket of ham-and-cheese sandwiches she and Willa had made to take to the Yoders'. "I'm coming!" she shouted. "Don't leave without me!"

Beth stood at the bottom of the steps, leaning on the banister, a look of boredom on her face. "No fear of that, I should think. This may take a while." She nodded in the direction of their other family members, all talking at once.

On the brick walk that led from the barnyard to the back porch, Eleanor, Jane, Willa and Cora had gathered around their father to try to convince him that there was no need to hitch up the wagon to go across the street. But for whatever reason, he wanted to take it and he wanted to drive. Each of the sisters there voiced their opinion on the matter while their father talked over them.

"*Dat*," Cora said, waving her hand. "It will take us longer to catch the horse out in the field and hitch him to the wagon than to just walk across the road."

"You don't drive anymore, *Dat*," Willa told him. "Remember? We've talked about this."

"I'm not going to be bossed around by women!" their father argued stubbornly.

Eleanor's voice could be heard above the din. "*Dat*, please be reasonable."

The only reason Henry and Jane weren't in on it was because Jane had one of her migraines and, even though she could certainly stay home alone, Henry had insisted she would remain behind with her. It was a perfect excuse for Henry, who didn't like social events where there was no work to be done. She was fine with a barn raising or a threshing party, but she was the one sister who'd been relieved when they'd stopped making social calls as a family when their mother had become seriously ill.

Henry didn't like social events involving Lavinia, a result of several encounters with the older woman before their bedridden mother had passed. Lavinia had come to the house with soup for the family but had insisted she see "her dear friend Aggie." Their mother and Lavinia had not been close, but more importantly, their mother had made it clear that she did not want anyone but her immediate family with her in her last days. While friends and neighbors may not have agreed with Aggie Koffman's choice, they had respected it.

Only Lavinia had come again and again, trying to wear the girls down. Henry, for whatever reason, had made it her personal responsibility to keep Lavinia out of the house and she and Lavinia had gone at it several times. In the end, Henry had won, but only because she was more stubborn than Lavinia. Lavinia had been the first visitor after their mother had died and had made a point of telling anyone who would listen that "she had been the first to see her dear neighbor after her passing."

"I'll be right back," Millie repeated and hurried up the steps.

She was flustered because nothing seemed to be going right today, a day she'd been looking forward to all week. Maybe her whole life. It had all started that morning when they couldn't find their father. Everyone had thought he was still sleeping because he often slept until someone woke him. It turned out he had risen before dawn and was in the cellar rearranging the canning jars of summer vegetables.

Then, when they all sat down for a breakfast of oatmeal, Millie had jumped up to get maple syrup and bumped into the table, knocking a pitcher of fresh cream over, sending a river of white across the table and into Eleanor's lap.

After breakfast, Millie had gone to put on her blue dress, only to find it missing. After questioning one sister after the next, none of whom seemed interested in her clothing crisis, she had discovered that Jane was responsible for the lost dress. Trying to be helpful to Eleanor, who was always complaining about the mountains of laundry, Jane had taken the dress the day before, and washed it in a load of clothes, but forgotten to hang them out. Millie had found her favorite dress at the bottom of the washing machine wrinkled and still wet. Jane had apologized and insisted Millie's dark green dress was just as nice but Millie had nearly burst into tears. She looked best in her blue dress and she wanted to wear it; she *needed* to wear it to Elden's house the way a toddler needed her security blanket.

In the end Millie had hung it on the line and

thankfully most of the wrinkles had come out and it had dried for the most part, though it was still a little damp at the arms. Which she realized now was making her chilly. Inside the house, she grabbed a sweater when she retrieved the basket of sandwiches, and when she came back outside, their father had relented and agreed to walk across the road rather than taking the horse and wagon.

By the time Millie came down the porch steps again, they were in the lane, headed toward Elden's. She scurried to catch up with Beth, who was carrying a jug of apple cider, bringing up the rear. "How did they convince him?" Millie asked, out of breath.

"Eleanor reminded him that it was Sunday and even animals needed a day of rest." Beth shrugged. "Then he just said *oll recht* and took off down the lane." She indicated their father out front and Eleanor and the others hurrying to catch up with him.

Millie smiled. "That was smart of her."

Beth shook her head as they followed their gravel lane toward the road. "Sometimes I think he argues with us just to argue. And to get Eleanor all worked up." She flashed a sly smile. "Because you know our big sister can get worked up."

Millie giggled, then realizing they were making fun of Eleanor, she sobered. It wasn't nice to make fun of people, especially on the Sabbath when their hearts were supposed to be turned toward *Gott*. "We shouldn't talk about Eleanor like this," she told her sister. "She does so much for us. She keeps the household running and worries about the money so we don't have to."

"Eleanor doesn't want us to know how worried she is about our finances," Beth said, keeping her voice low. "With *Dat* the way he is, he's not going to bring any income in anymore. His days of working as a mason are over. I overheard her telling Cora that we're going to have to figure out how to make money. Farming, even if we could do it ourselves, doesn't pay enough, not unless you're our neighbor." She indicated Elden's place. They were nearly to the county road now and once they crossed, they'd be in his lane. "I guess they owned two farms back wherever they came from."

"Wisconsin," Millie told her. They had caught up with their father and sisters but hung back to continue their conversation.

"Jane said she overheard Lavinia at the apple folic bragging about how well off her husband had left her and Elden. And Elden being the only boy, this farm is his to do with as he pleases. He's got plenty of irons in the fire. Apparently he's selling Christmas trees this year."

Millie hadn't really thought about Elden's financial situation, but, unlike most of the young men in Honeycomb who worked at a trade, he just worked his farm. She'd never really thought much about money because her parents had always provided for her. She felt bad that Eleanor was carrying that burden on her shoulders and hers alone.

At the end of the lane, Millie and Beth joined the others, and when it was safe, they crossed the road. As they walked toward the Yoders' house, Millie took in how neat Elden kept his two-hundred-acre farm. The land to their left where he had grown field corn for his stock had already been turned over, and winter wheat, a ground cover, had recently been planted. To the right was a pasture with a tidy, well-maintained fence and great patches of clover that had obviously been planted to give his horses a nice place to graze. The lane had just been leveled and he'd spread gravel to fill any holes that would prevent buggies and wagons from getting bogged down in wet weather. Their own lane had potholes in it and she wondered if she and Henrietta could *rett* it up before the fall rains came.

Halfway up the lane, Eleanor dropped back to speak to Millie and Beth. "I'll tell you the same thing I told the others," she said, looking a bit severe in her black church dress.

They weren't required to wear their black dress and white cape and apron on Visiting Sundays, and were free to wear what they *pleased* as long as it was neat and clean. At least Eleanor hadn't worn her white cape and apron, Millie thought. Eleanor was also wearing her black bonnet, which the rest of the girls had left home, opting for wool scarves tied over their organza *kapps* for warmth. Millie had chosen her dark blue scarf because she knew it looked nice with her dress.

"Each one of us will take a turn keeping an eye on *Dat*," Eleanor continued. "If it seems likes he's getting tired…"

As her sister went on, Millie's gaze strayed to the farmhouse coming into view. She'd been in the house over the years, but not in the last two or three. Unlike most Amish homes in Honeycomb, it wasn't an old-fashioned two-story farmhouse, but what her mother had said was called a Cape Cod. It looked sort of like a one-story house, only there were four big dormer windows and a sharply pitched roof. It had white vinyl siding and a huge front porch with two front doors, one in the center and one to the left in an addition. The center door led into a front hall and the other into a big mudroom and then the kitchen and pantry. When Elden's parents had bought the property, there'd been no house on it because the ramshackle farmhouse had burned down. Elden's father had built the Cape Cod with the help of neighbors he'd hired, including her father.

"Millie!" Eleanor grabbed Millie's arm, startling her. "Are you listening to me?"

She blinked. "*Ya.* I'm listening now."

"I *said* I don't know how long we'll be staying. You know how *Dat* is with strangers nowadays. He might feel uncomfortable." She lowered her voice. "Even scared. So keep an eye on him and be sure he feels safe."

The sound of a barking dog, Elden's bulldog, caught Millie's attention.

"Samson!" their father called, patting his pant leg. The dog that had been sitting on the front porch steps leaped down and raced as fast as he could toward the new arrivals.

Eleanor rolled her eyes but didn't say anything. She hadn't been thrilled when Millie had let their father go with Elden earlier in the week, but after their father had talked nonstop about Samson for two days, she'd relented and admitted maybe it had been good for him to be in the company of other men sometimes.

"Afternoon!"

Millie heard Elden's voice and turned to look for him. He was coming from the opposite direction of the house, waving. Behind him were three men, one Millie recognized as his uncle Gabriel, but the other two, who were closer to Elden in age, she didn't. His cousins, maybe? He'd mentioned that one or two of Gabriel and Elsie's children and their families might be there. There were also four little boys, the youngest maybe three, the oldest six or seven, dressed just like the men in dark pants, homemade denim coats and either a knit beanie or a black Sunday hat. Gabriel and Elsie's grandchildren, Millie assumed.

As Elden approached them, Millie smiled at him, waiting for him to make eye contact.

But instead of looking and speaking to her first, he called, "Good to see you, Beth. Sorry the weather isn't better." He slid his hands into his pockets and looked up at the sky. "Supposed to be sunny all day. I don't know where these clouds have all come from. Makes it chilly, doesn't it?"

"*Ya*, no sun will make it chilly all right," Beth replied. "Take this into the kitchen?" She raised the jug of apple cider.

"*Ya*. I was hoping we could eat outside. But *Mam* thinks it's going to rain. She wouldn't even let me set up the folding tables outside. We'll be eating in the kitchen." His gaze shifted to Cora and he nodded. "Cora."

"Elden." Cora smiled and headed toward the house.

Next he greeted Willa. "Glad you could make it. I heard JJ enjoyed your cookies last weekend."

Elden smiled at Willa as if there was a private joke between them, which made Millie feel like a third wheel on a two-wheeled cart. Here she was, smiling foolishly at him and he hadn't even looked at her.

"Elden!" their father called, clapping his hands to get the bulldog to leap and bark. "Tell these women that Samson and I are friends."

Still not looking at Millie, Elden walked toward their father and Eleanor.

"*Dat*," Eleanor said. "Please keep your voice down. No need to make a fuss. I just thought you might want to come inside and sit. It was a long walk here."

"Oh, it was not," he retorted. "And I'm not

coming inside with the women." He pointed at the fence where Gabriel Yoder and the two younger men were watching them with interest. "Men stand outside and we talk. Men stuff. Don't we, Elden?"

"Felty can certainly join us," Elden told Eleanor. "The women are inside putting together the meal."

Eleanor, looking severe in her black bonnet and three-quarter-length cloak, looked up at Elden, seeming none too pleased. "I thought *Dat* might want to rest."

"I'm not resting!" their father said, raising his voice again. The bulldog was standing at his feet, looking up at Eleanor as if pleading to let his friend stay out and play.

"*Dat*, it's cold, and—"

Their *vadder* gave a wave of dismissal and walked away, headed toward the other men. The dog followed.

Millie watched Elden as he chewed on the corner of his mouth and then, his voice low, said, "We're going to eat in twenty minutes or so, Eleanor. Then we'll all come inside." He met her gaze. "I'll keep an eye on Felty. He's fine."

Eleanor took a deep breath, her face tight with indecision.

"Let him go with the men, *schweschter*," Beth said impatiently as she walked past them. "How far can he go? Elden's with him."

Eleanor hesitated, then at last said, "Fine. But if it gets too cold out here before Lavinia calls you for dinner—"

"We'll all come inside," Elden promised.

Eleanor took another breath and nodded as if still trying to convince herself it would be all right. "*Danki*, Elden." Then she followed the sisters toward the house.

Realizing she looked foolish standing there, Millie headed in the same direction. "*Goot nummadag*," she said as she walked past Elden, her head down.

"Hey, Millie." He looked away from her. "*Nay*, Samson." He strode back toward the men. "No jumping, Samson. Off! Off! Felty, tell him to behave himself."

Millie tried not to be upset that Elden had talked to Beth…and to Willa and Cora and Eleanor, and not to her. He was, after all, hosting. He didn't have time to talk to everyone. Not with his uncle and cousins standing there watching them.

Millie's feelings were hurt, though. The way he had spoken to her the day he invited them to come over, Millie had thought he was inviting the family because he wanted her to visit. Which, she realized, looking back, was ridiculous. He was just being a nice neighbor. And now that he was ready to start having folks over and making rounds on visiting days, it was only logical that he'd invite them first. A way of easing back into it.

It all made perfect sense. But Millie's eyes still felt scratchy as she hung up her jacket in the mudroom and walked into the kitchen, a smile plastered on her face. "*Goot nummadag,* Lavinia," she said brightly. "Everyone."

The room was bustling with her sisters and the other women going this way and that with three little girls, dressed like the younger woman chattering in *Deitsch* as they folded paper napkins on a bench. Some of the women were setting the large farm table and the three plastic ones, all covered in tablecloths while others were removing lids and foil from various dishes lined along the long butcher-block counter that ran between the eight-burner gas stove with its two separate ovens and the large farmhouse-style sink. Because it was Sunday, the food had been prepared the day before. They really weren't supposed to cook at all on the Sabbath, but heating soup on a burner or popping biscuits into the oven wasn't really considered cooking.

"*Goot nummadag*," Lavinia said, barely looking at Millie. "Oh, Elsie! The corn bread. In the oven," she called from the far side of the kitchen.

Millie knew Elden's aunt, Elsie, though not well.

"Not to worry," Elsie, dressed as Lavinia and Eleanor both were, in black dresses, said. She grabbed a dish towel and opened one of the ovens.

"Not that one," Lavinia fussed, flapping her hands. "The other one."

Elsie said nothing, but obediently opened the other oven door and slid out a tray of corn muffins.

Millie stood in the doorway, her basket of sandwiches in her hand, not sure what to do. She'd be happy to help, of course, but was afraid to ask Lavinia what she needed because she was obviously already stressed. It was always better to make oneself busy and not pester their hostess, her mother had often said.

One of the two young women Millie didn't know walked past her, carrying a baby on her hip. The woman who looked to be around Millie's age stopped. "Hi, I'm Marybeth Kertz,

Gabriel and Elsie's daughter." Petite with dark hair and rosy cheeks, she smiled up at Millie.

"Um, I'm Millie Koffman," Millie said, noticing that not only did Marybeth have a *boppli* in her arms, but she was expecting another. "I live…*we* live across the road."

"Ah, Elden's friend. I'm so glad you could—" She looked over her shoulder in the direction of the little girls. "Sarey, please don't tear up the napkins. Fold them nice. Your cousin Bernice will show you. *Danki*, Bernice." Marybeth looked back at Millie. "Do you want me to take those?" Holding the baby in one arm, she pointed at the basket hanging on Millie's elbow.

Millie looked down at the basket. "*Nay*, I can put them out. I just wasn't sure…"

Marybeth leaned closer so that only Millie could hear her. "So Aunt Lavinia doesn't fuss at you." She smiled conspiratorially. "I know. She can be scary. Best way to handle it is to put whatever you've brought out without asking her." She looked up with big brown eyes. "That's how my sisters and sisters-in-law do it."

Millie nodded, looking down at the baby in her arms. She was a sweet thing in a long white dress, a yellow pacifier in her mouth.

She watched Millie with big brown eyes that looked like her mother's.

"And who is this *boppli*?" Millie asked, smiling at the baby.

"This?" Marybeth bounced the baby that was maybe six months old on her hip. "This is our Lizzy. Aren't you?" she crooned to the baby. "And Sarey is ours, mine and Jakob's. And we have a little boy, Thomas. He's outside with his *dat*. Likely chasing Aunt Lavinia's chickens." She shook her head. "The boy loves to chase chickens. I don't know why." She looked at Millie's basket. "What did you bring?"

"Um…" Millie looked down, then at Marybeth and shook herself mentally. She was being silly about Elden not talking to her. Her expectations had been misguided by her own imagination. He hadn't said anything to her to suggest he was interested in her as a potential girlfriend. Men like Elden Yoder didn't date and certainly didn't marry big girls like her.

Millie decided then and there not to give Elden another thought. For months she'd been wanting to go visiting the way they had when their mother was alive and she was here and she was going to enjoy herself. "Ham sandwiches," she told Marybeth. "Little ones. On slider rolls. Have you seen them in the grocery store?"

Marybeth's eyes widened with excitement. "I love those little rolls. We use them for hamburgers when Jakob makes them on our grill. I thought the small burgers would be better for the little ones." She wrinkled her freckled nose. "But I like them, too. Just the right amount of bread to burger."

Marybeth's smile was infectious, and Millie's mood lightened. Elden had done nothing wrong. She had no right to be upset with him. He had been neighborly, and she had somehow misinterpreted his meaning. Yes, he had said he wanted to spend time with her, but he obviously hadn't meant it in the way she had hoped. And that was that.

Millie needed to enjoy the afternoon and not worry about Elden. *Don't fret over the things you can't control. Let them go*, her mother had always said. *Trust in Gott and His ways.*

And Millie decided to do just that.

Millie thoroughly enjoyed the communal meal, and was reminded again of how much she had missed Visiting Sundays. The Sundays where there was no worship was a time to relax and enjoy the friendship and fellowship of her Amish community. It was a reminder to be thankful for all *Gott* provided each day. As was often done in Amish households when there were multiple guests, the women sat separately from the men to eat. Lavinia presided over the two folding tables that had been set up for the women and children, while Elden, his uncle, the two younger men as well Millie's father sat together at the oak farm table.

Millie didn't mind not sitting with the men because if she had, she'd have spent the entire meal trying not to look at Elden. However, as she ate, talking to her sisters and her new friend Marybeth and Marybeth's sister-in-law, she decided that if she ever married and had a home of her own, she would insist men and women sit together at a meal. Segregation made sense to her when men wanted to stand at a fence and talk crops and hoof infections and women wanted to talk babies and quilting. But that type of segregation came naturally. In this case, Lavinia had been adamant about the seating, not wanting her son to sit with so many attractive young women of marrying age, Millie suspected. So the women talked among themselves, as did the men.

Once the delicious meal of soups, sandwiches, salads and such was done, the men took their leave, going back outside while the women cleaned up the kitchen. Eleanor had briefly tried to get their father to stay in, but he refused and had quite merrily joined the other men. As Elden left the kitchen, he told Eleanor not to worry about her father because he'd be with him.

Once the kitchen was *rett* up, Lavinia suggested the women all move into the parlor to chat while Elsie's daughter and daughter-in-law nursed their babies. As Millie sat, listening to the various conversations, she tried not to be disappointed in the day. Even though it hadn't turned out as she had hoped, it had still been wonderful. It had felt good to be out of the house and she had made a new friend. She and Marybeth had hit it off so well that Marybeth had asked her to stop by one day in the coming week. Only a year older than her, Marybeth had insisted it was lonely at home all day with her little ones while her husband, a framer who worked for a construction company, was gone all day. She said he worked five days a week, and sometimes even Saturday when the Mennonite contractor he worked for was busy.

After Marybeth had fed her little Lizzy, she asked Millie if she'd like to hold her while she took her three-year-old to the bathroom. Cuddling the baby on her shoulder as she drifted off to sleep, Millie was surprised by the emotions that welled up inside her. She had never thought much about having babies of her own. Maybe because she had told herself no one would ever marry her. But holding Marybeth's *boppli*, she felt almost a physical desire to have one of her own. Where had that come from, she wondered.

"Mildred?"

Millie looked up to see her father standing in the doorway to the parlor.

"Sorry to disturb," he told the other women, holding up his hand.

"What do you need, *Dat*?" Eleanor rose from a chair near the woodstove that was providing just enough heat in the room to make it cozy but not hot. "Are you tired? Are you ready to go home?"

He looked at Eleanor. "Not going home yet." He returned his gaze to Millie. "Walking down to the pond to see a dock. Elden built it. Want to come?"

Marybeth squeezed past him in the doorway, her daughter following behind. "I'll take her," she said to Millie, putting out her arms. "*Danki*. Oh my, she's sound asleep, isn't she?"

Millie carefully passed the baby back to its mother, wishing she could have held her a few minutes longer and breathe in her sweet, milky scent as Lizzy slept. But if she didn't deal with their father, Eleanor was likely to march them all home, and Millie wasn't ready to go yet.

"Come on, Mildred," her *fadder* said, hooking his thumb in the general direction of the pond. "Taking Samson for a walk. Going to see the dock. I like a dock to fish on."

"*Dat*, maybe you should sit down and rest a while," Eleanor said.

Their father cut his eyes at his eldest daughter, giving her the look they had all known from their childhoods. *Dat* had always been easy to get along with. He'd been kind and set a good example in everything he said and did, but when he'd had enough of bad behavior or whatever earned his disapproval, he made his point with one look. The one he was directing toward Eleanor.

Eleanor sat back down.

"*Ya* or *nay*?" Felty asked Millie.

"Um…" Millie started across the parlor, glancing at Eleanor then back at their father. "Sure, *Dat*. I'll go see the pond."

"The *dock*," he corrected, then turned

around and walked back through the house the way he'd come.

Millie heard the back door close before she entered the mudroom to collect her coat and wool scarf. As she turned the corner, she nearly walked right into Elden. She gave a cry of surprise, then pressed her hand to her heart that was suddenly pounding. "Sorry." Embarrassed, she kept her head down. "I didn't realize you were here. My father—" She pointed to the door that led onto the porch. "He…he wanted me to walk down to the pond with him."

"With us," Elden said. "Which one is yours?" He turned to the women's coats hanging on hooks.

"That one," she said, pointing, thinking it had to be obvious. Hers was twice as big as anyone else's.

Elden plucked it from the hook. "This your scarf?"

She nodded, not sure what was going on. Why was Elden here? Had he been waiting for her? It seemed like it.

Elden handed both to her and watched her slip on the coat, close it with the hook and eyes, and then tie her scarf carefully over her *kapp*. As Millie knotted the scarf under her chin she realized she should have been smart like Eleanor and worn her Sunday bonnet, which was made to fit over a starched prayer *kapp*.

"Temperature has dropped outside," Elden said, watching her. "You bring a neck scarf?"

She shook her head. "I was warm enough when we walked over."

"*Ya*, but days are getting shorter, aren't they?" He moved along the row of hooks on the wall, looking for something. He stopped and grabbed a dark blue knitted scarf. "Here, wear this. It will be chilly out near the pond."

He walked back to her and offered it.

"It's *oll recht*, I don't need—"

He lifted his brows and the look on his face made her fear he might try to tie it around her neck if she didn't take it. "*Danki*," she said softly, lowering her gaze as she accepted it. Then she quickly wrapped it around her neck. It was well made and the wool wasn't in the least bit itchy. "Nice scarf," she mumbled.

"*Mam* made it for me. She's good with knitting needles." He opened the back door and looked down at her. "Ready?"

Still not quite sure what was going on, Millie followed him out onto the porch. None of the other men or boys seemed to be around, but her father was already halfway across the barnyard. He was headed north toward the pond, the bulldog trotting happily beside him.

Elden walked down the steps and she followed him. "Gabriel and his son and son-in-law are out in the shed checking out my new brush hog," he said.

She frowned. "I thought those kinds of big mowers were pulled behind a tractor. I don't know about your bishop, but my uncle would never approve of a tractor."

He smiled slyly at her. "Bishop Paul is a good man, but no, I can't own a tractor." He held up a finger. "I can drive one for an *Englisher* if it's required for work I get paid for, but I can't own one. Last spring when *Mam* and I went to Lancaster County to visit an elderly aunt, I saw a horse-drawn brush hog and decided I could use one here, what with all the land I still want to clear. Bought an old brush hog at auction and put a 15 horsepower engine on it. I hitch my cart to Clyde, my Clydesdale. I know, not an original name," he said with a smirk, "and I pull the brush hog behind the cart. I've still got a couple of adjustments to make, but I think it's going to work just fine."

She smiled at him. "That's clever. You figuring all that out."

He shrugged. "I like a challenge."

He looked at her when he said it, but then he kept eyeing her until she felt awkward and scanned ahead for her father. Her *dat* had stopped under an apple tree that was missing most of its leaves and he was making a little pile of sticks while the dog sat watching his every move. "What is he doing?" she wondered aloud.

Elden watched for a moment. "Ah, a jump."

"A jump?"

"My fault. I showed Felty how I was teaching Samson to jump over sticks and such." He shrugged. "Just for fun. And maybe to vex my mother." He pointed in her father's direction. "And now Felty's trying to get Samson to jump over all sorts of things. Don't worry. Samson won't jump anything higher than a woolly bear."

Millie laughed, trying to imagine the dog jumping over the thick, fuzzy black-and-orange caterpillars. "I can ask him to stop," she said.

"It's fine. Felty's enjoying himself." He looked at her again. "How about you? Having a good time?"

"Um, *ya.* I am. It's nice to get out. And to spend time with neighbors. Friends." It was on the tip of her tongue to ask what was going on.

Why her father had come for her. Why Elden had been waiting, but she couldn't think how to phrase it, so she didn't say anything.

"Me, too," he said, sliding his hands into his pockets as they walked. "I'm having a good time. A surprisingly good day." He was quiet for a moment and then went on. "Sorry about sending your father in for you. I didn't know how it would look, me walking into my *mam*'s parlor and asking you if you wanted to go for a walk. I figured this way was safer. And your *dat* really did want to see the dock I built."

Millie felt her heart skip a beat. *He had sent her father in for her? So she could go for a walk with him?* This couldn't be real. It couldn't be happening. She felt a little out of breath, not because of the pace at which they were walking, but because the obvious conclusion was that…that Elden *did* like her. Why else would he want her to go for a walk with him?

Then she felt a sense of panic. *Unless maybe he was interested in Beth and he wanted to ask Millie about her.* Beth was the one he had spoken to first when they arrived.

"I wanted you to come walk with me—" Elden hesitated. "Because I wanted to ask you—"

Millie heard her father cry out and looked up to see him lying on the ground. *"Dat!"* She took off at a run.

Chapter Eight

"Dat!" Millie cried again, running toward him.

The way she took off surprised Elden. Typically, Amish women her age didn't run. For many, it was considered inappropriate. His mother certainly would have said so if she'd seen her. But Millie was not a typical young Amish woman, was she?

Elden had forgotten how fast she could run. In their school days he remembered that despite her size, she had always been picked for softball teams first, certainly before him. Everyone wanted her on their team because she could run fast and hit the ball over the fence into the Swartzentrubers' field where their schoolhouse was located. Millie had been so athletic that he'd been intimidated by her.

"*Dat*! Don't get up," Millie hollered, waving her arms at him.

Elden bolted toward Felty. Samson was barking as if to alert them that the older man had fallen. By the time Elden reached Millie and her father, the bulldog was standing over Felty, licking the older man's cheek. Her father's glasses were lying in a pile of dead leaves beside him.

"Samson, back up," Elden ordered.

Millie fell to her knees in the wet grass and picked up his glasses, which appeared unbroken. There had been a rain shower outside while they were having dinner and everything was wet. *"Dat?"* She reached out as if wanting to touch him, but not knowing where for fear he'd been seriously injured. He was lying facedown. *"Dat,* can you move?"

Elden went to his knees on the other side of Felty. "Catch your breath," he said calmly.

"Dat, can you hear me? I asked if you can—"

"*Ya, dochter,* I can *move,*" Felty sputtered. He tried to push the bulldog off as he rolled onto his back.

"Samson, off!" Elden ordered sharply.

"Where are my glasses? Lost my glasses." Felty tried to sit up, bracing himself with his hands.

"Here they are." She slid them onto his face. "*Dat*, I think you should lie still," Millie fussed. "You might have broken your leg or arm. Maybe I should call an ambulance. I imagine someone here has a cell phone." While cell phones, like many other modern conveniences, were frowned upon in their Old Order community, the truth of the times they lived in was that families needed a cell phone, if not for work then to be able to place a call in an emergency.

Felty blew a raspberry at his daughter and sat up without assistance.

"*Dat!*" Millie cried, her tone reprimanding.

It was all Elden could do not to laugh. The older man couldn't have been hurt too badly to have that sort of sense of humor.

Millie brushed some dead grass off his face. "Can you move your legs?"

Felty kicked one leg out and then the other, demonstrating he could move just fine. "Stop your fussing, *dochter*. I tripped. I didn't fall off the top of a windmill!"

"How about your arms?" Millie ran her hand over her father's denim coat sleeves, one and then the other, brushing off bits of wet leaves and brown grass.

Felty flexed one arm and then the other.

"Fine. See?" He reached out and stroked Samson's muzzle as the dog poked his nose at him. "Just a tumble, right, boy?"

"*Dat*, what were you doing? Did you fall walking?" She looked at Elden, the worry plain on her pretty face. "He's never been unstable on his feet before." She returned her attention to her father. "Did you get dizzy?"

Felty frowned and looked to Elden, extending his arm in silent request. Elden rose and took the older man's hand, helping him to his feet.

"Can you imagine what my life is like, Elden? It's this times seven." Felty pointed to Millie. "Yack, yack, yack." He was wearing fingerless cotton gloves, and he opened and closed his hand so that it looked like a bird's mouth.

"What happened, *Dat*?" Millie, still on her knees on the ground, asked again.

Elden picked up Felty's black, wide-brimmed Sunday hat, banged it on his knee to get the grass and leaves off and handed it to him.

"I didn't fall over like a *boppli*." Felty's tone was indignant. He pulled his hat down over his head. "I was showing Samson how to do it."

"Do what?" Millie asked.

Millie made to get to her feet, and before

Elden thought better of it, he grabbed her hand to help her. As her hand touched his, he was surprised by a warm feeling that surged through him. Her touch, warm and soft, somehow made him feel...like everything was going to be all right for him. It felt so good that he hated to let go when she pulled her hand away.

Felty exhaled, getting more perturbed by the moment. "I was showing Samson how to jump over the little fence I made." He pointed at a small bundle of sticks in the grass that Elden hadn't noticed before. "I made a fence jump and he wouldn't go over it so I was showing him how."

Millie crossed her arms. "You thought you and that stumpy-legged dog were going to jump fences? What? Stick fences today, stockade fences tomorrow?"

"Maybe," Felty answered indignantly.

Elden had to press his lips together not to laugh.

But Millie didn't. She threw back her head and laughed hard, a big belly laugh that made her eyes water.

And Elden's heart melted. He wanted to ask her to the harvest frolic. He had nearly gotten up his nerve, but then Felty fell. He took a deep breath. What if she said no? Could he take the rejection now, when he was only just climbing out of the depths of disappointment and self-doubt?

"*Oll recht, Dat.*" Millie finally stopped laughing. "I think it's time we went home." She looped her arm through his and they started toward the yard.

The bulldog and Eden followed.

"What if I'm not ready to go home?" Felty asked, walking beside his daughter.

She tilted her head and gave a great, overblown sigh. "Then I'll have to tell Eleanor that you want to stay, even though you fell for no obvious reason."

Elden caught up to them and walked on Felty's other side. He wanted to ask Millie here and now about the frolic, but with her father there, that didn't seem wise. If she said no, he'd rather not have anyone else witness his embarrassment.

"I told you!" Felty blustered. "I was showing Samson how to take the jump."

Millie shook her head. "I don't know if Eleanor is going to accept that. She may not believe you. She may think you made it up to keep from getting into trouble with her."

"What would make her think that?"

"I don't know, *Dat*. Maybe because the other

day when you were trying to make bird feeders with pine cones and peanut butter and seeds and you got peanut butter all over the counter and on the floor, you told her you were making a peanut butter sandwich. Even though there was bird feed on the counter and the floor."

"I like feeding the birds," he grumbled. "Birds have to eat, too, and I like watching them from my chair in the living room."

"I know you do." She stopped. "But I don't know how Eleanor's going to respond." She looked at him cheerfully. "So do you want me to go tell Eleanor we're ready to leave or should I tell her how you—"

"I think it's time we go home," Felty interrupted. He offered his hand to Elden and shook it warmly. "Thank you for having us. Hope we can return the favor, neighbor."

"I'll go round up the girls. It's time we got home to check on Jane, anyway." Millie's gaze met Elden's for a split second, and she smiled warmly. Then she walked away.

Elden watched her go and decided he was going to invite her to the frolic. If she said no, then she said no.

But he wouldn't ask her today. Maybe tomorrow. The following day at the latest.

But he would definitely ask her.

* * *

Wednesday morning after the breakfast dishes were cleared, Eleanor walked into the kitchen where Millie and her sisters were still tidying up, and clapped her hands together. "Applesauce day," she declared. "We've put it off long enough. It's a perfect day for it." She glanced out one of the big windows.

It was overcast and threatening to rain. When Millie had gone out to milk before breakfast, she'd been chilled by the time she brought the milk back into the house.

"*Ya*, I agree. A perfect day to make applesauce," Millie piped up when no one said anything. Since Sunday she'd been in a contemplative mood. She needed something to distract her from thoughts of Elden that swirled in her head.

She was so confused. Did he like her or not? She'd been upset when he barely spoke to her when they arrived at his house the other day. But then later, he'd sent her *dat* inside to ask her to go for a walk with them. With *him*. So maybe he did like her. Or maybe he only wanted to speak to her alone so he could ask about his prospects with Beth and had never gotten the chance before their father had taken his tumble.

Or perhaps he really *was* interested in Millie. Would that really be such a crazy idea? She was smart and resourceful, a good cook, decent at sewing and she was a woman of deep faith. So what if she was fat? She wasn't so fat that she couldn't do her chores or that she couldn't run when her *dat* had hurt himself. And *Gott* had made her this way, hadn't He? Which meant, she lectured herself, that she was good enough for any man, even Elden.

That was what she kept telling herself. On Monday she had hoped Elden might stop by to say hello. When he didn't, she thought he might come Tuesday. Today she'd woken up wondering if she had imagined the connection she'd felt to him on Sunday when they had taken a walk. With an inward sigh, she pushed those negative thoughts aside. There was no sense dwelling on them. *Gott* was good and He had a plan for her. Even if it wasn't the plan she was hoping for. And she had to make herself content with that.

"Love to help make applesauce," Henry said, stuffing the last piece of toast in her mouth as she headed out of the kitchen. "But I told Anna Mary I'd have a look at her stove. She says it's not working and with her being widowed and her boys living so far away, she doesn't know who to ask. She's been cooking on her old woodstove." Her last words were mumbled as she made a quick retreat.

"I'd help, but I promised Liz I would help her with her wedding chest," Willa announced, following Henry out of the kitchen. "Henry is going to drop me off. The wedding is only a month away," she threw over her shoulder. "I'll be home by supper."

"Wait!" Jane called, closing the refrigerator door. "Can I go with Willa? While she helps Liz, I can visit with Susie. Please, Ellie?" she begged, already starting to take off her dirty apron.

Eleanor, who had been busy wiping down the counter, turned around. "Who's going to help me make this applesauce?"

"Sigh so gude, schweschter? Plee-ase?" Jane, who they sometimes forgot was still a teenager, begged.

"Let her go. I'm here to help," Millie said. "I don't have anywhere to be. And Cora and Beth can help, too. That's four of us. Plenty of cooks in the kitchen." She placed her hands on her hips and glanced at the huge copper-bottomed pots that Henry had brought into the kitchen from the cellar. "It will be fun, just the four of us."

Eleanor hesitated and then with a sigh, said, "Fine, Jane. Go. See your friend."

"Danki!" Jane threw her arms around her eldest sister, gave her a hug, and raced out of the room.

"Do you two want to start carrying in the apples?" Cora, who had been reading a book at the kitchen table, asked. "We've got a lot of peeling and cutting to do before they're ready for the kettles."

"Sure," Eleanor agreed, seeming already frazzled although the day had barely begun.

"I'll help carry them in," Millie offered.

Bushels of Black Twig, Granny Smith, Winesap and Jonathan apples they had picked at the Masts' orchard the week before waited on the porch. Making applesauce with her family was something that Millie looked forward to all year. She loved picking apples. And she loved the heady smells of cooking apples and cinnamon and seeing the results—rows and rows of quart jars of applesauce lining the pantry and cellar shelves. There was something so satisfying about knowing that a few days' work provided good food that would last them until the next fall and the next crop of ripe fruit.

So the four remaining Koffman sisters began their task. The baskets were heavy, but

Millie had done manual labor since she was young, and she didn't mind the lifting. Peeling was easy. Her fingers remembered what to do while she sat and chatted with her sisters. As the minutes, then hours, ticked away in the cozy kitchen, they laughed and jumped from one subject to the next. It was all great fun until Cora reminded Millie what she was struggling with.

"Sooo…" Cora drew out the word. "I saw you and Elden through the window on Sunday, Millie." She carried another big bowl of clean apples to the kitchen table. "How was it?"

Millie concentrated on the Black Twig apple she was peeling, keeping her gaze down. "Fine."

Cora glanced at Beth and the sisters exchanged looks. "What we were wondering is, does he like you?" she asked with a giggle.

Suddenly Millie felt anxious. Cora wasn't one for giggling. She was probably the most serious of all of them. Had she and Beth been talking about her and Elden? "I… I don't know if he likes me."

"Elden is a good-looking man," Beth declared, turning from the stove where she was stirring a pot of apples, water and sugar. "And single."

"*Very* single," Eleanor agreed, not looking up from her peeling. "He'd make a fine husband," she added.

"I have an idea. I think we should go to the harvest frolic," Beth said. "And then Elden can ask Millie to ride home with him." She looked to Eleanor. "Do you think we could go? Everyone is talking about it. There's going to be singing and games and a bonfire and they're going to roast marshmallows."

"Are they making s'mores?" Cora looked to Eleanor. "I'll go if there are going to be s'mores."

"I don't want to go to the harvest frolic," Millie said, continuing to peel an apple. "And Elden is not going to ask me to ride home with him."

"I think he is. Because he likes you." Beth sang her last words as she took a long-handled wooden spoon and scooped up a spoonful of cooked apples to taste.

"Well, I think he likes you, Beth," Millie blurted, startling them all, including herself. "He came right over to talk to you Sunday when we arrived." Flustered, she stood up and, in the process, dropped apples from her apron onto the floor.

Beth made a face. "He does not like me. You're the one he asked to go for a walk with him. I think he sent *Dat* in to ask you so his mother wouldn't know."

"Makes sense. Since she ruined his last betrothal," Cora pointed out.

"We don't know that to be true," Eleanor chimed in as she cut a peeled apple into chunks and dropped them into a bowl in her lap.

Millie pressed her lips together as she stooped to pick up the fruit she'd dropped. "Can we talk about something else?" One apple had rolled under the table and she had to get down on her hands and knees to retrieve it.

"No one would blame you if you set your *kapp* for him," Eleanor said. "Elden Yoder is a good catch. I think you two are well suited to each other."

"Is that what all of you are talking about behind my back?" Having captured the apple, Millie rose to her feet and set it on the table. "That I've set my *kapp* for Elden? Because that isn't true."

Beth and Cora exchanged meaningful looks.

"You never know," their oldest sister remarked, not looking up. "Sometimes even a smart woman is the last to see what's plain as day to everyone around her."

"Plain as day," Millie muttered to herself a

short time later as she came up the cellar steps, carrying two cases of quart-sized canning jars.

She knew Eleanor hadn't meant the comment unkindly, but it was upsetting. Maybe because Millie desperately wanted to think that Elden *was* interested in her. She wanted to believe that there was a chance that he could fall in love with her, because if she was honest with herself, she was already half in love with him. She knew it was ridiculous, but she'd felt that way since they were kids. Not all the boys had been kind to her at school. There had been the jokes about what she packed for lunch, comments about the shape of her body and the laughter directed at her, but Elden had always been kind.

At the top of the cellar steps, Millie set down the boxes and turned to lower the metal Bilco doors. It was cold and gray, and drops of icy rain were beginning to hit her as she eased the door down.

She remembered being in the third grade, sitting outside for lunch on a sunny day in May. Elden had been in the fourth grade. There had been picnic tables that one of the neighbors had built so the students could eat outside under the trees. She'd been sitting with Annie, whom she'd been friends with for as long as she could remember, along with some other girls. There had been a bunch of boys, including Elden, at the next table over. Millie had left her lunch on the table to fetch a cup of water for her and Annie from the well. When she came back, she'd unwrapped the peanut butter and honey sandwich her mother had made for her. She'd nearly taken a bite before she realized there was something sticking out of it that didn't belong. When she opened the sandwich, she found that someone had stuffed a bunch of grass and leaves inside it. Then one of the older boys, an eighth grader named Alvin, began to oink.

Millie had been so mad that she got up from the bench.

"I'm sorry," Annie had whimpered. "I didn't know how to stop him."

But Millie hadn't been angry at Annie; she was furious at Alvin. She'd marched over to the rude boy. "You think that's funny, ruining someone's lunch?" she'd asked him, hands on her hips.

Alvin had sniggered. Other boys at the table had joined him.

"That's just mean," Millie had told him.

Alvin had stood up and he was a lot bigger

than she was, a lot taller. He'd leaned down and oinked right in her face.

That was when Millie had drawn back her fist with the intention of hitting him right in the nose. She didn't care if she was going to be in trouble with their teacher, or her parents, or the bishop, or even *Gott*. But just as she was about to throw the punch, Elden had appeared at her side and placed his hand on hers, lowering it gently.

"Not worth it," he'd whispered in her ear. "Here." He'd pushed a sandwich, still in a plastic baggie into her hand. "It's ham and cheese with mustard," he'd told her. "The spicy kind. A *goot* sandwich."

And then he had walked away, and Millie had gone back to sit with the girls. And she had never forgotten how good Elden's sandwich had tasted.

Millie dropped the second cellar door with a bang and picked up the cases of jars. She had almost reached the back porch when she heard a dog bark. A bark she was familiar with, now. She groaned. It was Samson, and if Samson was there, that meant Elden was there, too.

He'd probably stopped by to ask Beth if he could take her home from the harvest frolic.

"Millie," Elden called out.

She ignored him. She didn't know why. She'd almost reached the back door when she heard his footsteps on the porch steps.

"Millie!"

She spun around. "*Ya*, Elden." She held the jars against her. "What is it? I'm busy."

"H-hi." He slid his hands into his pockets but kept his gaze on her. "I... I see you're doing some canning."

"*Ya*." She looked down at the jars. "Applesauce."

"Mmm. I love applesauce."

She watched his dog trot up the steps so she didn't have to look at him.

"Uh...anyway. I... I was wondering if you—" He looked at his boots, then up at her. "If...if your family is going to the harvest frolic this weekend."

"I don't know," she said, wondering if she just ought to ask him straight out if he wanted her to send Beth out to talk to him.

"It... It sounds like it's going to be nice. I... I'm going and I was wondering if you... if I could take you home after," he said all in a rush.

Millie's heart skipped a beat. *He wanted to take her home.* Which made it practically a date because that was how it worked in Honeycomb. Single men and women of marrying age met and got to know each other at singings and frolics and social gatherings, and if a boy was interested in a girl, it was tradition that he asked to take her home.

But did he really want to take her home or was this some sort of ploy to…what? She didn't know. Make Beth jealous? Or maybe he liked Willa and just was afraid to say so because she was so pretty.

"I don't think so, Elden." She turned away. "My sisters are waiting for the jars."

"Millie—I—" He took a breath. "Why not?"

She turned to look at him. "If you want to go out with Beth, you should just ask her. Or I can, if you want me to."

He frowned. Samson had moved between them and was now looking up at his master almost quizzically. "What are you talking about?" Elden made a face. "I… I don't want to take Beth home. I mean, she's nice and all but—"

"If you're not interested in her, then why did you talk to her instead of me when we arrived on Sunday?" she demanded.

"What?" He was still acting as if he had no idea what she was talking about.

Millie shifted the cases of jars in her arms.

It was beginning to rain in earnest now. She could hear the pitter-patter on the tin roof of their porch. "Sunday. You walked right over and said hello to Beth and…and talked to her. And then you talked to Cora and you barely looked at me. You barely said hello to me and then off you went."

He shook his head slowly. "Millie, Beth was in front of me. It would have been rude not to speak to her. I didn't get a chance to talk to you because I knew your *dat* wanted to stay outside with the men and if I didn't get him—" He lowered his voice, she guessed in case any of her sisters could hear them from inside.

He took a step closer to her. "If I didn't walk your *dat* over to where the other men were, he'd have been stuck in my mother's kitchen with all the women. And I know that isn't what he wanted."

"Really?" she asked. "That's why you didn't talk to me?" She wanted to believe him.

"*Ya.* Why would I make something up like that? When you arrived, I wanted to ask you about the harvest frolic, but there was no chance to talk to you alone when we ate, not with my mother listening to every word I said. And then when you came outside, when we were walking, that's when I was going to ask you, but then Felty fell and…" He gestured with one hand and went silent.

The bulldog looked up at Millie.

Millie exhaled. "I have to go inside."

"Does that mean yes?" One side of his mouth rose in a half smile. "You'll ride home with me?"

"It means no such thing. I'll have to see if we're even going." She shrugged. "Who knows." She met his gaze. "Maybe someone else will ask me to ride home with them."

The look on his face told her he couldn't tell if she was joking or not. In truth, she didn't know, either.

"I suppose you better ask me again at the frolic." She turned to the door.

He reached around her and opened it. "Really? You're not going to just say yes now?"

"Nope," she said. "Have a good afternoon, Elden."

Then Millie walked into the house and closed the door behind her with her foot. She entered the kitchen carrying the jars and said with a big grin, "I'm going to the harvest frolic. Anyone else want to go?"

Chapter Nine

Elden set down his fork. He'd eaten only a few bites of scalloped potatoes floating in curdled cream and a half a corn muffin. He'd nibbled at the fried pork chop that was dry, even with all the canned gravy his mother had poured over it. After working himself into a headache, he didn't have much of an appetite. And he had more on his mind than eating.

He'd been surprised by Millie's response when he'd gone to her place to ask if she'd like to ride home with him from the harvest frolic. More than surprised. Maybe a little hurt. He thought she'd say yes. If he hadn't thought so, he wouldn't have had the courage to walk over and boldly ask her. He'd thought she liked him.

Maybe he wasn't meant to court. Maybe he wasn't meant to marry, he told himself.

But if *Gott* didn't mean for him to take a wife, why would He have put the desire in Elden? Elden had always wanted a wife and children. He thought he could be a good husband and father. Was he wrong?

"*Sohn*, you barely ate a thing."

Elden pushed his plate away, giving up even the pretense of eating. Usually he could eat whatever his mother made. He was used to things being too salty or a little burned, but tonight he didn't have it in him.

His mother's forehead wrinkled with concern. "Are you feeling sick?"

Elden shifted back in his chair, wiping his mouth with a paper towel. "*Nay*, I'm not sick. Just have a little bit of a headache."

"You got soaked this afternoon. You could be coming down with something."

"That's not how it works, *Mam*. The rain can't make you sick."

"You sure it's just a headache? What if you've caught the flu?" She rose, leaned over and pressed her palm to his forehead. "You feel a little warm to me. You running a fever?"

"*Nay*, no fever." He leaned back, out of her reach. He wasn't a child anymore and he didn't like it when she acted as if he was.

She returned to her chair. "Earlier, you went across the road to the Koffmans'. I saw you."

He looked at her. "You're spying on me?"

"It's not spying if I look out my own window and see my own son walking down my own lane." She gestured with her fork. "Then back again. Why did you go to the Koffmans'?"

He had half a mind not to tell her and, worse, to lie. But he wasn't that person and he never wanted to become that person. "I'm thinking about going to the harvest frolic on Saturday."

"You are?" She smiled. "I think that's an excellent idea. It will be a good way to get your feet wet again. Start setting your intentions on a nice girl. I hear half the unmarried girls in the county will be there." Finished with her pork chop, she picked up her last bit of biscuit and started to sop up the gravy on her plate. Then suddenly her brow furrowed. "Wait. Why did you go to the Koffmans'? You wanted to tell them you were going to the frolic?"

He exhaled heavily. He didn't want to have this discussion with her. But here he was. "To ask Millie if I could take her home afterward." He met her gaze, almost daring her to make a comment. But after what had happened with Mary, he doubted she would. Since the

breakup, she'd walked a fine line with her remarks concerning his situation as a single man.

His mother pursed her lips and dropped the
leftover biscuit onto her plate as if she'd suddenly lost her appetite as well. She got up and
began clearing away the dishes, but her silence
and the pained expression on her face was an
obvious sign of her disapproval.

Elden rose. "Can I help you clean up?"

She shook her head. "This is my job, *sohn*.
It's the least I can do, being a widow and de-
pendent on your charity."

Elden bit back the retort that this farm was
hers as long as she lived, and that he loved her
and would never consider her a burden. He'd
said that many times before. Instead, he returned the buttermilk to the refrigerator.

There'd never been any doubt in Elden's
mind that his mother loved him and wanted
what was best for him. But this time around
he was going to do this his way. If Millie *did*
like him—which he wasn't even sure about
now. But if she would be willing to walk out
with him and get to know him, he was going
to keep his mother out of it. Because he really liked Millie. Even when she was standing there on her porch, telling him she didn't

want to ride with him, he still wanted to talk to her, to be with her.

It had crossed his mind when he walked home from the Koffmans' that maybe this was the same situation he'd had with Mary. He realized now that he had liked Mary far more than she had ever liked him. When he added his mother into the equation, he wondered if things with Millie would end the same way they had with Mary.

But Millie hadn't said she absolutely wouldn't ride home with him. So he still had a chance.

And as scary as it was, he liked Millie enough to think she was worth pursuing. Chewing that over, he headed for the mudroom.

"Where are you going?" His *mam* followed him, a dishrag in her hand.

"Out to my shop. I'm going to start making those frames for the wreaths. Another week and it will be November. I've got orders from both greenhouses in Hickory Grove and I imagine it won't be long before they're selling Christmas decorations. You know those *Englishers*." He put on his hat. It was already dark outside, but he'd run a generator for light, and if it got chilly, he had a kerosene heater in his shop. A lot of evenings he sat in the living room with his mother and read or paid bills or something while she knitted. While she talked. But he wasn't in the mood for her chatter tonight. "By Thanksgiving weekend, they'll be wanting to buy wreaths to hang on their doors. It's too good an income making frames for the wreaths and such not to do it."

Like many Amish men, he did a variety of things to bring money into the household. He raised some crops, he sold firewood he cut himself, he sold extra vegetables they grew, and this year he was going to sell Christmas trees.

"*Ya*, Christmas will be here before we know it," his *mam* agreed.

Elden thought on that on the walk to his workshop in the dark, Samson trotting beside him. For most Amish, gift giving wasn't a big part of Christmas. The day was celebrated with devotions and a quiet meal with family and sometimes friends. But it had always been a tradition in their home to give each other something. When he was a boy, he'd wished for things: a new sled, a puppy, a baseball and bat.

He wondered if he could wish for Millie's hand in marriage.

* * *

As it turned out, the entire Koffman family went to the harvest frolic at the Beachys'. Even Henry, who avoided social events, especially ones intended for unmarried men and women to mingle with the ultimate intention of finding a spouse. Parents weren't specifically invited, but when their father heard there was going to be a bonfire, he'd been so excited that no one had had the heart to tell him he wasn't supposed to go. Rather than disappointing their father, Eleanor had talked to Alma Beachy, who had insisted that Felty and Eleanor were welcome at the frolic as they could use as many chaperones as they could get. They were expecting a big crowd.

Millie and her family took two buggies that evening, which had been Eleanor's idea. That way, she and their *dat* and Jane could go home when he got tired, leaving the second family buggy for the other sisters to take home. Should any of the older girls be asked to ride home with a boy, that would be just fine, too. Millie hadn't been sure if that comment had been directed toward her or Willa, but didn't ask for fear that simply by saying it aloud it wouldn't happen for Millie. She was already worried that she had ruined her chance with

Elden by telling him no when he asked. She didn't know what had come over her, speaking to him that way. Maybe she'd just been scared.

She was certainly scared now as she crunched on a peppermint Annie had handed her as they stood in the ever-growing shadows, watching the Beachy boys—and there were nine in all—stack the wood for the bonfire that would soon be lit.

There must have been fifty or sixty people on the Beachys' property, most of them young and single. That included the matchmaker's gaggle of white-blond girls with black prayer *kapps* all coming from an Amish community in Wisconsin and staying with Sara Yoder in Seven Poplars, in the hopes of finding a husband. The matchmaker had brought several young men from out of town with her as well.

All around Millie and Annie there were girls walking around in groups of two and three, giggling and blushing. The boys tended to group together this early in the evening as well. Six or seven of them were throwing a football behind the chicken house and several had joined in to prep the bonfire. Alma and Fred Beachy, along with other chaperones, hung back, manning refreshment tables or sitting together among themselves, closer to the house. The idea of the chaperones was to keep behavior at a level acceptable to the bishops, while allowing the young folks to mingle and get to know each other. According to Alma Beachy, at least one marriage had come out of every annual harvest frolic they'd sponsored since they began having them six years ago.

"There's Elden again. See him over there?" Annie nudged Millie. "Near the fence. I think he's looking this way."

Millie turned to search for Elden and Annie pinched her. Millie yelped. "Ouch! What was that for?" Millie murmured under her breath. She rubbed her arm. "That hurt."

"You're not supposed to look at a boy who's looking at you," Annie admonished.

Millie had seen Elden twice already. The first time, he'd waved to her as he was tying up his buggy and she'd lifted her hand in greeting but kept walking. Then he'd started to approach her after the group singing, but she'd grabbed a tray of sandwiches and headed in the opposite direction toward the refreshment tables. She didn't know why. Maybe she wanted to be sure he really wanted to talk to her. If he did, he'd keep trying, wouldn't he?

"Don't you know anything?" Annie whispered.

"I don't know anything about dating," Millie said in exasperation. She was chilly. Beth had said to wear her cloak, but she'd chosen her navy blue going-to-town jacket because it went so nicely with her blue dress. Which she was wearing again even though it wasn't Friday. "How would I? I've never had a beau, same as you. I've never even been asked to ride home with someone before."

For a few minutes they stood side by side watching everyone. They spotted Willa with JJ, standing rather closely to each other. Then they'd giggled over Millie's sister Henry marching up to one of the older Beachy boys and telling him he'd never get the fire going stacking the wood like that. She'd then started bossing them all around, making them take the pile apart and rebuild it.

Millie was so happy to be at the harvest frolic. Things had been hard in the months leading up to their mother's death from kidney disease and then it had seemed as if they'd all been in a fog for a whole year. Now, at last, she felt more like herself again. She still missed her mother terribly, but just as so many people had told them, the pain wasn't so sharp anymore, though it was still there. Millie felt like she could breathe again and as if everything might be all right.

"Hey, do you know who that is?" Annie lifted her chin in the direction of a young man around their age walking toward the bonfire.

He had to have been a full head taller than any of the other boys there. Millie didn't think she'd ever seen such a tall Amish man before. He was wearing a hat that looked slightly different than the ones all the men wore in Kent County. His coat was different, too. It had buttons on it, whereas because they were a conservative community, their coats only had hooks and eyes. "Never seen him before," Millie said.

Grinning, Annie gave Millie a little push. "Cute, isn't he?" She nibbled on her lower lip. "Come on." She grabbed Millie's arm and dragged her toward the bonfire, which one of the Beachy boys was just getting ready to light. Under Henry's direction.

Annie walked right by the tall boy and then at the last moment *accidentally* bumped into him. Ten minutes later, Millie found herself still standing with Annie while she talked to the boy who they learned was Abe Kertz, a cousin to the Beachys, visiting from Ohio.

As Millie listened to them chat, she watched Elden move from the fence, where he'd been talking to a couple of young men, over to a picnic table where her father and Fred Beachy were standing. She smiled as she watched Elden interact with her father. Elden was so kind to him and her father lit up whenever he was around.

Millie returned her attention to her friend and the young man. They were talking about Abe's father's turkey farm and how many thousands of turkeys they sold to *Englishers* during the Thanksgiving and Christmas holidays. As the conversation continued, Annie seemed to be enjoying Abe's company so much that Millie wondered if she ought to excuse herself.

"I've got you trapped this time," a male voice said in Millie's ear, startling her.

She'd know that deep voice anywhere and she whipped around. There Elden was, dressed like all the other men in dark pants, clean work boots, a shirt and suspenders with a coat. But unlike most of the others, he wore a dark beanie pulled over his head. Hand-knit by his mother, she suspected. But he didn't look anything like the other young men milling around. Not to Millie. To her, he was by far the most handsome.

"I'm not going to let you dodge me again," he warned, his tone teasing.

"I'll talk to you later," Annie said, squeezing Millie's arm. "Good to see you, Elden."

She and Abe walked away, living Millie alone with Elden.

"I was not—" Millie met his gaze as he lowered his chin, the look on his face telling her there was no denying it. "*Oll recht*, maybe I was avoiding you a little bit," she admitted.

"And why is that?" He looked around to be sure no one was close enough to hear their conversation. "Is it because you don't—you're not—you don't want to know me better?"

Millie was surprised by his forwardness. *Nay*, his honesty. She hesitated. Did she give him another flip answer and walk off? Her response the other day seemed foolish now, especially because she desperately *did* want to ride home with him. She liked Elden. She *really* liked him.

But was there any sense in spending time with him, getting her hopes up? Because they would only be dashed. She knew that.

She met his gaze, not sure what to say.

"Just tell me the truth, Millie. If you really want me to go, I'll go. But—" He went quiet for a moment and then said, "But I don't think you want me to. I think you enjoy talking with me as much as I enjoy talking with you. I think you'd like to at least consider riding home with me tonight."

His blue-gray eyes held hers and she swallowed hard, her mouth so dry that she wished she had saved the peppermint Annie had given. Before she had a chance to speak, Annie walked back over.

Annie glanced at Elden, then at Millie, then at Elden again. "I'm going to borrow Millie for a second," she told him. "Don't move." She grabbed Millie's arm and pulled her away. "Did he ask you to ride home with him?" she whispered when they were a distance from him.

Millie nibbled on her lower lip. "He said he'd leave me alone if I wanted him to. But he said he thought I liked him and that he didn't really think I wanted him to leave me alone."

"Okay…" Annie drew out the word. "That's good, *recht*? A man who says what he thinks. How he feels." She grabbed both of Millie's chubby hands between hers. "Millie, this is what you've been waiting for. He wants to get to know you better."

Millie groaned. "I know. Right in front of all these people," she said voicing her fears aloud. "Which means by tomorrow afternoon everyone in Honeycomb will know. Including his mother, and I already know she doesn't like me."

"I don't think that's true, but who cares about Lavinia?"

"I imagine Mary did when she sent her packing."

Annie frowned. "You need to work on your confidence, *fryn'd*."

Millie ignored Annie's comment about self-confidence because she could only handle one problem at a time right now. "What about when he changes his mind? When he decides he doesn't like me?" Her lower lip trembled. "Or he finds someone skinnier or prettier or... *Ach*, I don't know," she fretted.

Annie sighed. "Nothing in this world is guaranteed but death and *Gott*'s love for us. And mice in your larder," she added with a wry smile. "That's what my *grossmammi* always used to say." She studied Millie for a moment, then laid both her hands on Millie's shoulders, looking into her eyes "What have you got to lose? He's not asking you to marry him. He wants to take you home in his buggy. He probably cleaned it all up and gave his horse a few extra brushes. You going to let that go to waste? And what about Elden? Maybe *he* needs this. Ever consider that? Can you imagine how terrible he must have felt when his mother ran his betrothed off?"

"So that is true?" Millie asked. "It's not just gossip."

Annie shrugged. "Knowing Lavinia, it's possible." She let go of Millie. "So spend the evening with him. Ride home with him. What's the worst thing that could happen? Nothing might come of it, but you'll have had a fun night with your handsome neighbor. I'd ride home with him in a second if he asked me."

Millie nodded. "You're right. I should just enjoy his company."

"*Ya.*"

"And…and if nothing comes of it," Millie said, thinking if she said the words aloud, she could convince herself. "Then at least I'll have ridden home with a boy for the first time."

"Exactly. So go on. And I'll talk to you tomorrow after church."

"*Danki*, Annie. You're a good friend," Millie said as Annie walked away.

Millie found Elden standing closer to the fire, his bare hands out for warmth.

"*Ya,*" Millie announced to him, stretching out her own hands.

His forehead crinkled. "*Ya* what?"

"Yes, I'll let you take me home."

He broke into a grin. "You will?"

"Well," she said. "Probably. But first I'll have to see your marshmallow-roasting skills."

"Oh, I can roast a marshmallow," Elden told her, a twinkle in his eyes. "And I can make the best s'more you've ever eaten. The marshmallow is toasted perfectly, so that the chocolate melts. Just thinking about it makes me want one."

Millie laughed and then realized he was still looking at her. Watching. "What?" she said.

He shrugged. "I was thinking how I like the sound of your voice when you laugh. It's so joyful. So genuine."

Millie didn't know what to say, because no one had ever said anything like that to her before. Certainly not a boy. But as it turned out, she didn't have to say anything because her father strode over to them with a big bag of marshmallows in one hand and saplings to use for roasting sticks in the other.

"You two look like you need some marshmallows," her father said, stopping in front of them. "What do you say, *sohn*? Going to make your girl a s'more?"

"*Dat*," Millie whispered, mortified. "I'm not his girl."

Elden didn't act as if he had heard the older man. If he did, he was too polite to say anything.

Her father ignored Millie's correction as he held out the bag to her. "Get a couple." He glanced around as if looking for someone, then said, "Don't tell your sister but I'm saving some for later." He patted his coat pocket, fat with marshmallows.

Millie made a face. "*Dat*, you can't carry marshmallows in your pocket." She fished two out of the bag for her and Elden while Elden grabbed two sticks. "They'll melt and get all sticky."

"Not if I eat 'em first, they won't," he countered, then he walked away leaving them both laughing.

It was after eleven when Elden steered his buggy up the Koffmans' driveway. A three-quarters moon hung low in the sky, so bright it lit their way. The temperature continued to drop outside and puffs of white frost rose from his gelding's mouth. But despite the cold, it was warm inside the buggy thanks to a space heater he ran off a car battery. As they made their way closer to Millie's house, he wished her driveway was longer. He wished she'd lived farther away from the Beachys'. He wished the night wouldn't come to an end.

It was time he got her home before her sisters or father began to worry about her, though. And they'd already taken the long way home. After they made s'mores at the frolic, they'd ended up sitting on a bale of straw near the bonfire and talking. And the more he talked to Millie, the more he liked her. She was so open. And funny. And smart. And she didn't just let him talk. She had plenty to say, and not once all evening was there an uncomfortable silence between them.

Riding home, as Millie chatted about her childhood and how wonderful her mother had been, it occurred to Elden that even though he had been sure six months ago he would never fall in love again, suddenly the possibility was there. It was right there beside him on the buggy seat. Millie was sitting so close that he could have reached out and touched her hand if he'd dared.

"I'm sorry," Millie said as the buggy rolled to a stop near her back door. "I've been talking your ear off."

"*Ya*," he teased, the moonlight coming through the windshield of the buggy so that it illuminated her face. "And I've enjoyed every word."

She looked at him and he noticed that a lock of blond hair had fallen from her *kapp* to curl at her temple. Her cheeks were rosy and her lips made him think of ripe strawberries in the summer sun. He wondered what it would feel like to touch that curl.

"Are you teasing me?" she asked. "Sometimes I can't tell when you're teasing or being serious."

"I'm serious." He couldn't stop smiling. "But in a teasing way."

"Well," she said, bringing her hands down soundly to her legs. "I should go. I'm sure Eleanor is waiting up for me. Likely watching us from the kitchen windows." She hesitated and when she spoke again, her voice softened. "Thank you for the ride home, Elden. I really had a good time."

"A good enough time to go out with me tomorrow night?" he asked before he lost his nerve.

"*Nay*," she said.

"*Nay*?" he asked in surprise. "Why not?"

Her eyes widened as if it was the silliest of questions. "Because tomorrow is a church Sunday and both of us will be busy all day. We'll be at the Masts' and you… I think Alma Beachy said they were having church tomorrow. She said with everything all *rett* up already, why not have another crowd tomorrow?"

He pressed his hand to his forehead. "You're right. Tomorrow is church. And Monday *Mam* has a doctor's appointment and I told her we could go shopping after. She doesn't like taking the buggy into Dover on her own. And Tuesday I promised my uncle Gabriel that I would— Wednesday," he said quickly. "How about if we do something together on Wednesday?" He tried to think fast. "I… I'm making wire frames for wreaths for some of the greenhouses nearby. I have to drop some off at the Millers'." He held his breath because tonight he'd had a better time than he could remember in a very long time. Maybe better even than when he was with Mary. "If Wednesday won't work—"

"*Nay*. Wednesday is good." She smiled at him as she reached for the door. "I have chores in the morning, but how about one thirty?"

"I'll be here to pick you up," he said.

"Sounds good." She slid her door open.

Elden watched as she landed gracefully on her feet.

"Good night, Elden," she said, looking up at him.

He sat there until she went into the house and then he drove the short distance home, smiling all the way.

Chapter Ten

A month flew by so quickly that Millie barely
had time to catch her breath. One day she was
riding home from the harvest frolic with Elden,
then the next they were officially walking out
together.

A week after they started seeing each other,
Elden had taken her father for a ride into town
to buy some lumber and had asked him if he
might court his daughter. When they returned,
Millie had been waiting nervously at the window, unsure of how her father might respond.
She never knew how he would react to anything these days. Sometimes he woke up his
old self, his mind clear, and sometimes he
woke confused, and there seemed to be no
rhyme nor reason to it. To her relief that day,
when the men came up the lane, she couldn't

tell who was grinning harder, her father or her new beau.

After that, she and Elden saw each other nearly every day, not just attending social events, but sometimes they would go for a walk, or he would ride into town with her and her father to get groceries or go to an appointment. It was the kind of courting she had imagined since she was old enough to dream of meeting and marrying a man and having a family of her own. Elden was sweet and attentive, and they talked a lot, sometimes about trivial things, sometimes important things. They talked about their favorite ice cream, about what it meant to them to be Amish. They discussed the sermons they heard on Sunday and wondered if the Almanac was going to be reliable that year. Were they really going to get a lot of snow?

One thing Millie and Elden hadn't done was have supper with his mother at their place. Elden and Lavinia occasionally came to the Koffman home to share a meal, but usually at Millie's father's insistence. Millie got the distinct impression Elden was keeping his mother and her apart, and while she kept thinking she should bring it up, somehow she couldn't do so. The same went for the subject of his betrothal to Mary. While he mentioned the girl in passing a couple of times, Millie got the idea he didn't want to talk about her. She'd always let the subject drop even though she wanted to know the details, because what if he was still in love with her? She didn't know if she'd be able to bear it if he was.

Midmorning on the day after Thanksgiving, Elden pulled onto the Koffman lane, wooden crates of wire frames to make wreaths, garland and table sprays from greenery stacked above his vehicle's wagon wheels. Millie was going with him to deliver them to Miller's greenhouse in Hickory Grove, five miles from Honeycomb.

By the time Elden pulled up near the back porch, Millie wore her cloak and a wool scarf tied over her head. Eleanor didn't approve of Millie being seen with Elden without a proper head cover, but Millie feared her prayer *kapp* might blow away and her black wool church bonnet was too much for such a casual outing. Beneath her cloak, she wore a blue dress, one of three she now owned because Willa, after saying she was tired of seeing her in the same dress every day, made her two more from fabric they'd discovered in their mother's sewing room.

"There you are," Elden said. He started to get down from the wagon to come to the door but settled back on the bench seat when he saw her.

Millie smiled. Her heart sang every time she saw his handsome face. How had she been so blessed to have him as her beau? "Here I am." She grasped an iron handhold and stepped up into the wagon. When they'd first started dating, he'd kept trying to help her in and out of his buggy, but she'd reminded him that it wasn't really the Amish way and they didn't need folks talking any more than they already were.

Willa and Jane kept Millie up-to-date on what people were saying in Honeycomb about her and Elden. Words like *mismatched* and *odd couple* were thrown around their community, but Millie tried not to pay any attention to it, although a part of her was still waiting for the romance to fall apart. Sometimes she had nightmares that he broke up with her to court Willa, Beth or even her friend Annie. But by day, she enjoyed what she had with him and tried not to worry about the future.

Millie settled down on the bench seat beside Elden.

He lifted a wool lap blanket and covered

her with it. "Hot brick at your feet. *Mam* said it might snow today. It's been years since we had snow this early in the season."

"*Ya*, the sky does have that color to it, doesn't it?" Millie said, looking up. She breathed deeply. "I think it smells like snow, too."

"I hope the ride isn't too cold for you. Sorry we couldn't do this in the buggy, but there was no way all of this would fit inside and I want to bring some greenery home to decorate the house. I thought you might like some, too. Maybe some pine boughs in the windowsills inside because they smell so good."

"I'd love that. We always used to decorate the windowsills with pine boughs. They make the house smell so good."

Elden slid his hand across the wagon seat and took hers, and even through their knit gloves, she could feel his warmth and tenderness. When they held hands, it was all she could do not to think about what it would be like to wake up each day to see his smiling face.

"Ready?" he asked.

"*Ya*."

Elden took up the reins, murmured gently to the giant workhorse and off they went down the driveway.

"How was Thanksgiving at Gabriel's?" she asked as they waited at the end of the lane for cars to pass.

"It was nice. Quiet."

She nodded because it had been a quiet affair at their house as well. They'd fasted, as was the family's tradition, until supper when they'd a simple meal of white bean soup and fresh bread. They'd spent the day together talking, reading and knitting or mending with several breaks when their father had led them through devotions.

When Millie and Elden pulled into the gravel parking lot of Miller's greenhouse, which it shared with Miller's harness shop, the place was packed. There had to be at least a dozen parked cars, trucks and minivans as well as a horse and buggy and a wagon full of fresh greenery tied to a hitching post. *Englishers* crisscrossed the parking area, carrying armfuls of red and white potted poinsettias and big, beautiful wreaths made from pine boughs, holly leaves and mistletoe, all constructed on Elden's frames.

"My goodness," Millie said, her breath coming in puffs of white. "Look at all the people."

"*Ya*, Joshua Miller and his sister Bay's business has really taken off." He eased the Clydesdale in beside the other wagon and jumped out to tie it up. "Bay married a Mennonite, David Jansen, and they live down the road a piece."

Millie climbed down from the wagon seat, lowering her voice. "She left the order and her parents allow her to their home?"

He shrugged, walking around the horse to Millie. "They do. I know many don't allow *lost* children to come home, but I'd like to think that my *mam* wouldn't shun me if I chose to leave the church."

"*Ya*," Millie said, unable to imagine leaving her Amish life behind. "But that's not something you ever considered, is it?" He never suggested he was unhappy in the life he had been born into, but this wasn't something a couple who was courting should keep from each other. Even though she and Elden had not specifically spoken of it yet, once a couple was openly courting, the assumption was that their intention was to wed. Millie couldn't imagine marrying a man who wanted to leave his Amish life—and take his family with him.

"*Nay*, I've never considered it." He halted in front of her, rubbing his hands together for warmth. "I choose the life *Gott* has chosen for me." He frowned. "You?"

She shook her head emphatically. "I love my

life as an Amish woman." *And I love you*, she thought. But she didn't say it out loud because what if he didn't feel the same way about her? Or what if it was too soon to say the words? For the hundredth time she wished her mother was still alive. This wasn't a subject Millie felt she could discuss with Eleanor, but she could have with her *mam*.

Elden gazed into her eyes and she felt a brush of cold on her cheek. She looked up into the sky and saw that it was filled with snowflakes slowly fluttering downward to settle on the dead grass, the wagon and Elden's eyelashes. Seeing the snow and standing so close to him as he looked down on her, she felt a little lightheaded. It was such a perfect moment, feeling the warmth of his body so close to hers, and seeing the emotion in his gray eyes, she wanted it to last forever,

"*Goot*," Elden said softly. "We're of the same mind. I think that's important for a couple." He hooked his thumb in the direction of the greenhouse. The door to the shop was decorated in greenery, and a large sign painted in red and green read Christmas Shop Open. "Let's see if we can find Joshua or Bay and make this delivery." He headed for the door and she fell into step beside him.

An *Englisher* woman in a red coat came out the door carrying two enormous white poinsettias, with a little girl of four or five, who followed carrying a small white poinsettia.

Millie smiled as they went past, then followed Elden inside. The shop was small with a checkout counter and a passageway that led into a greenhouse that must have been thirty or forty feet long and filled with red and white poinsettias. Inside, it was warm and loud and filled with *Englishers* all trying to pay for their purchases.

"Wow, I didn't expect the place to be this busy," Elden said, gazing around. "I don't see Bay or Joshua. I'm going to go see if I can find one of them. You *oll recht* here?"

She nodded. She was enjoying the commotion. *Englishers* and their ways fascinated her. She didn't want to be one, but she certainly liked observing them. "I'll wait for you here."

Flashing a smile, her handsome beau gingerly made his way through the crowd toward the greenhouse.

Millie stood where she was, looking at all the wreaths and sprays hanging on the shop walls. Some of the arrangements were simple, something she would hang on their door, and others were elaborate with sparkly ribbon and plastic birds stuck to them. One wreath that was two feet across had sparkly, white fake poinsettia leaves wired to the greenery. Another had big silver bells hanging from it. She gazed in the direction Elden had gone and spotted him talking to a pretty Amish woman who looked to be maybe twenty. She was smiling up at him, giggling.

Millie's face fell. Was that Bay, the one who had married a Mennonite? The way she was flirting with him, Millie doubted it. That was a single woman trying to catch the attention of a single man.

Millie knew she shouldn't be surprised. Elden was what her mother would have called a catch. He was handsome, well set financially, and never been married. Any girl in the county would be happy to have his attention.

Millie watched to see if Elden was flirting back. He was smiling, but he didn't do anything to encourage her. After a moment the girl pointed and Elden nodded, said something more and then headed back toward the shop.

"We're going to drive around back," he told Millie when he reached her.

Outside, where it was still snowing, they got into the wagon and he drove around the back of the greenhouse, where there was a second greenhouse. The owner Joshua, or co-owner, as Elden explained, met them along with several teenage boys, and the crates of wire frames were quickly unloaded. Joshua gifted them a huge pile of fresh greenery and soon Elden and Millie were on their way again.

They rode maybe half a mile, the snow drifting around them, making the familiar landscape appear even prettier than usual. "You're quiet," Elden said. "Feeling okay?"

Millie clasped her hands together. She'd been so happy riding over, so happy for weeks, but seeing the woman flirt with Elden had brought all her self-doubts crashing down on her. "Do you know her?" she asked.

"Know who?" They rolled to a stop at a crossroad. There were no cars coming, but he didn't urge the Clydesdale forward.

"The woman you were talking to in the greenhouse. The pretty one in the rose-colored dress."

He frowned, his eyes scrunching at the corners. She watched carefully. Was he going to deny he'd even talked to her?

"Katie?" he asked.

"Is that her name?"

Elden turned to her. "That's Katie. She works

for the Millers. Sometimes she's in the harness shop, sometimes in the greenhouse."

"She's very pretty.'

He shrugged. "I suppose so."

Millie hesitated. "Is she someone you'd be interested in courting?"

He looked at her as if she had just said the silliest thing. "Millie. I'm courting you. Remember?"

She looked away, watching a blue pickup truck stop at the four-way crossroad. Christmas music floated from the driver's open window.

"She's younger than I am. Skinny and pretty. I can understand why you might be interested in a girl like that. It's only natural that a man—"

"Millie, I've told you before. I like you just as you are. In fact, I don't *just* like you, I—" He went silent, his Adam's apple bobbing, then continued. "You need to have more confidence in yourself. In us." A car pulled up behind them and he pulled into the intersection. "I think we need some hot chocolate. I brought some. And marshmallows." He tapped a paper bag at his feet. "I know your *dat* loves hot chocolate with marshmallows. How about we go back to your house and make some?"

She looked at him for a long moment. He was right. She knew he was right about having more confidence, but it was so hard when he was so handsome and so perfect.

And she wasn't.

"*Ya*," she said, watching the snow settle on the horse's back. She wasn't comfortable talking to him about why she worried she wasn't good enough for him. If she gave him all the reasons, she was afraid he'd realize she was right. He was too good for her. So instead, she ignored his comment about her self-confidence and forced a smile. "Let's have some hot chocolate. And I made some cookies. I was fiddling with recipes for the cookie exchange at my aunt's house next weekend. You're still coming, right?"

"We are. I wouldn't miss a chance to spend the evening with my sweetheart." He covered her hand with his, and Millie made the decision to stay in the moment and not worry about Katie or girls like her.

At least not today.

When Millie walked into her aunt Judy's kitchen the following Saturday, carrying her white chocolate chunk cranberry oatmeal cookies, she spotted Lavinia right away. The older woman was busy setting her rice cereal bars on a plate at the kitchen table. And if she was here, that meant that Elden was there because Lavinia rarely took the buggy out herself and she certainly didn't dare leave her property with snow on the ground. Millie must have missed him outside in the sea of buggies when her family had arrived.

"Afternoon," Millie greeted Lavinia and her aunt, who was pouring sugar into a big crockery sugar bowl. She didn't meet Lavinia's gaze as she rested the cookie tray on her hip. "Where should I put these?" she asked her aunt. "On the table?"

Looking flustered, Judy snapped the lid on the sugar canister. "We've got tables set up for the exchange in the sitting room. Those are for eating." She indicated the kitchen table with plates of cookies on them. "The Bishop insisted we be able to sample the goods." She flashed a wry smile.

It was their family's inside joke. Uncle Cyrus was turning out to be an excellent bishop, but having come to the position only recently, it was important to him that his new status be recognized by everyone, including those closest to him. Instead of referring to him by his first name, Aunt Judy had taken to calling him

The Bishop as if it was his name, though not when he was within hearing distance.

Millie set her tray on the table so she could grab one of the empty serving plates. "I'll leave some here and put the others in the sitting room."

As Judy walked into the pantry, Lavinia moved to the end of the table and peeled back the foil on Millie's cookie tray. "What are these?"

Millie moved some of the cookies onto the plate. The plan was to enjoy cookies and coffee and tea and milk for the children, then they would have the cookie exchange. Everyone was supposed to bring six dozen of one kind of cookie, then you could take up to six dozen different cookies home with you. "White chocolate chunk cranberry oatmeal cookies."

Lavinia wrinkled her nose. "What's that all over them?" She pointed.

Not sure what she meant, Millie leaned over to look. "Oh, white chocolate I melted and drizzled over it." She smiled at Elden's mother. "So they look pretty. And Christmassy."

Lavinia frowned.

"I've never heard of such a cookie." Lavinia sniffed.

"I didn't exactly follow a recipe." Millie

shrugged. "I thought about what would be good in an oatmeal cookie and threw it in. The dried cranberries are pretty and the white chocolate makes me think of snow. Timely with this early snowfall," she added, sounding more cheerful than she felt.

For weeks she'd been telling herself that it was her imagination that Lavinia didn't like her, but she was coming to the terrifying conclusion that it was true. Elden's mother was never outright rude to her, but Millie always felt a sense of disappointment whenever Lavinia spoke to her. She couldn't help worrying that Lavinia saw what Elden didn't. That she was fat and ugly.

"I don't care for dried cranberries." Lavinia wrinkled her nose. "Too tart. And the red is showy. Not properly Plain like an oatmeal cookie with raisins."

Millie didn't like the face Lavinia was making. If Lavinia didn't like cranberries that was one thing, but Millie got the feeling that Lavinia was trying to make her feel bad about what she'd brought for the cookie exchange.

"I don't think my Elden likes dried cranberries, either."

Millie felt her face growing warm. Her first thought was to respond, "Well, he doesn't have to eat them," but instead, she plastered on a smile, scooped up her tray of cookies and excused herself as her aunt walked back into the kitchen.

On her way to the sitting room, Millie greeted friends and neighbors and children racing through the house with a smile. As instructed, she left her tray on one of the tables laden with tins, baskets and plates of cookies. Right now, all the women, girls and small children were inside while the men chatted outside. Aunt Judy would soon call the men in. Which meant that if Millie wanted to catch Elden alone for a few minutes, this might be her only chance.

Near the front door Millie dug through the pile of wool cloaks to find hers and went out the door. The steps were slippery and muddy from the snow and so many people going in and out of the house, and as she took the last step her feet went out from under her and she fell hard. Looking around, afraid someone had seen her, she used the handrail to pull herself up. Blessedly, while the barnyard was full of men and boys, no one seemed to have noticed her. Head down, she followed the sidewalk, brushing the snow off the back of her cloak.

Maybe she shouldn't have come at all today.

Maybe she shouldn't have made cookies that were so *showy*.

Maybe she should have told Lavinia that Lavinia didn't know what her son liked, because the previous day he had eaten seven of Millie's white chocolate chunk cranberry oatmeal cookies.

Maybe she should have—

"Millie? Are you all right?"

She looked up to see Elden striding toward her. "I saw you fall. I was afraid you'd hurt yourself."

She pressed her hand to her forehead. "*Ach.* I'm such a *doplich*." Fat *and* clumsy, she thought.

Elden stepped in front of her. "Millie, you are not. You're the most graceful—"

His voice caught in his throat and she looked up at him, surprised by the emotion she heard in his voice. All around them, men milled about, tying up their horses, talking crops and weather. Children ran in the lane, throwing wet snowballs at each other, but the sounds of the barnyard faded as she gazed at Elden's handsome face. She waited for him to finish what he was saying.

He had been looking down at his snowy boots, but he lifted his chin now to meet her gaze. "Millie, I had this whole thing planned out but—" He glanced around and seeing several men headed their way he grabbed her hand and walked around the corner of the house, leading Millie. He followed the shoveled sidewalk until they were out of sight of the others and then stopped and turned to her, still holding her hand.

She laughed nervously, thinking he was behaving oddly. "Elden, what are you—"

"*Sigh so gude.* Please." He took an uneasy breath. "Millie, let me say this before I lose my nerve. I had planned to wait, but I can't wait any longer. And I know we haven't been courting long, but I know what I want, and I think you want the same thing." Again, he took a breath. "Millie—" He met her gaze with his beautiful eyes. "Millie, will you be my wife?"

Millie gasped, pressing her hand to her heart, afraid it might stop beating. "Will I—" Now she was the one who couldn't catch her breath.

"I know I need to talk to your father, but considering the circumstances, I thought I better ask you first because—"

"*Ya,*" Millie heard herself say in a whisper.

But he hadn't heard her and he kept talking. "If the answer was *nay*, then there would be no need. But I hope the answer isn't no because I want to marry you. I love you, Millie, and—"

She rested her hand on his coat, feeling dizzy. He loved her. *He said he loved her.* She found her voice, speaking over him. "*Ya,* Elden. *Ya,* I'll marry you."

"And I hope that—" He halted midsentence. "You will?"

Tears filled her eyes. She couldn't believe this was happening. *Ya,* she'd been dreaming about it, but she hadn't thought it would actually happen. She'd been sure that eventually he'd see her for who she was, what she was, and realize there were too many pretty, skinny *maedels* in the world to be bothered with the likes of her.

This was the happiest moment of Millie's life.

But that was all it lasted. One moment. And then the fear came back. He was saying he loved her. That he wanted to marry her, but he was right, they hadn't been courting very long. Not long enough for him to realize that he didn't love her. That he didn't want to marry her. And when he realized how he really felt, she'd be devastated. Mortified when everyone in Honeycomb found out he had broken up with her.

Think fast, she told herself. *Think fast, Millie.*

"*Ya*, I do want to marry you, Elden," she said. Because it was true. But then she tempered it with, "But, but you're right. We haven't been courting long. And, and I think we shouldn't tell anyone yet."

His brow furrowed. "Not tell anyone?"

She gave a little laugh. "Just not…yet." He looked so disappointed that she added, "Soon, but not yet. Our little secret to enjoy. Just until the New Year. Until Epiphany, maybe?" *Because by then you'll know what you really want*, she thought. And maybe it would be her. Maybe he did love her, but she needed him to be sure because she loved him so much. She didn't know if she could bear it if he broke up with her.

"Until Epiphany," he repeated, glancing away, then back at her. "*Oll recht*. I suppose I can wait. And enjoy the secret with you in the meantime."

"*Ya*." She gazed up at him and he put his arms around her and again she felt dizzy. It was the first time he had ever held her this way, and the scent of him was powerful. "It will be just between us. Our little secret."

"Our little secret," he agreed, his smile as big as hers.

Chapter Eleven

Sunday, after three hours of morning church services, including a ninety-minute sermon, Millie was the first to pop up from her bench on the women's side of the Koblenz sitting room and hurry into the kitchen. She felt guilty that her mind had wandered often during the preacher's sermon, but she couldn't stop thinking about Elden and his proposal. When she'd returned from the cookie exchange, she'd been bursting at the seams to tell her sisters and *dat*, but she'd kept her mouth shut to keep from spilling the news that still didn't seem real to her. Elden Yoder had told her he loved her. He had said he wanted to marry her.

Now, almost twenty-four hours later, she was wondering if she'd made a mistake in asking Elden to keep their betrothal a secret.

Thinking back, she realized that he'd shocked her by asking so soon after they began dating, and that had triggered her request. She'd said it because she was afraid he would change his mind. She feared he had asked on impulse and would think better of it later. But then, recalling his face when she'd said yes, she wondered if maybe this *was* all real. Maybe Elden *did* love her. She certainly loved him, although she hadn't told him for fear she'd start to cry and because she wasn't quite ready to give herself to the idea that he would become her husband. So many things could happen to change his mind. Wasn't it a kindness to give him a chance to think it over before they told their families and friends?

"What do you want me to do?" Millie asked Adalaide Koblenz who was stirring two pots of soup on her woodstove at the same time.

"*Ach*!" the tiny, round woman said. "I've been up since four and still everything isn't ready. You'd think as long as Amos and I have been having services in our home, I'd be better at this." She set down the wooden spoons. "There are tables set up in the parlor. While the men move the benches in the sitting room, could you put glasses at every setting and be sure there's silverware? Everything's in the pantry."

Millie grabbed the work apron she'd left on a peg in the kitchen and dropped it over her head, covering her Sunday best black dress and white cape and apron. "*Ya.* Don't worry. It will all be fine," she assured her hostess as she cut across the kitchen. "My *mam* always said that hungry men were easily pleased."

"Aggie was a woman wise beyond her years," Adalaide called as Millie walked into the pantry.

Inside the small room of floor-to-ceiling shelves, Millie found the extra silverware and glasses. Annie was there, pulling rolls out of a plastic bag and adding them to bread baskets for the tables.

"I thought that sermon would never end," Annie groaned.

Millie slid a serving tray off a shelf above her head and began loading it with glasses from a crate that had come from the church wagon full of communal tables, chairs and dishware.

She filled the tray with glasses as quickly as she could. While she and her sisters hadn't hosted church since their mother's passing, she knew how stressful it could be even for an organized woman like Adalaide, so she was eager to help her. As she grabbed another tray to load it with silverware, she realized Annie was watching. "What are you looking at?" Millie asked.

"You. I don't think I've ever seen you smile like that. And your face. You look so bright and happy." Annie moved closer. "What's going on with you?"

Millie fully intended to say, "Nothing," but that wasn't what came out of her mouth. As she turned to her best friend, she whispered, "He asked me to marry him."

Annie squealed and threw her arms around Millie. "You're getting married!"

"Shhh," Millie hushed, holding out her hand.

"Oh, Millie," Annie went on. "I'm so happy for you. When did he ask you?" She grabbed Millie's arms, squaring up to her. "I want to hear every single word he—" Her gaze moved suddenly to the pantry doorway and her eyes got round.

"What?" Millie whispered.

Before Annie could respond, Millie heard her sister Jane say, "There you are. Adalaide said to help you set tables."

Millie grabbed the closest tray of glasses and whipped around, handing it to Jane without making eye contact with her. "I'll be right in." She pretended to count silverware until her sister walked out of the pantry.

"Do you think Jane heard me?" Millie whispered, grabbing Annie's arms.

Annie stared wide-eyed at her. "I— Oh, what does it matter! You're marrying Elden Yoder!"

"Please keep your voice down," Millie hushed. "I didn't tell them yet."

"You didn't tell your family?" Annie whispered.

Millie bit down on her lower lip. "*Nay*, we agreed to wait."

"Millie!" called Adalaide from the kitchen. "When you finish with that, can you run down to the cellar and grab six jars of spiced, canned peaches?"

"*Ya!*" Millie hollered through the door. "I'll get them." She looked back at Annie. "I'll tell you everything later." She grabbed the second tray of glasses. "*Ach*, I just hope Jane didn't hear me," she groaned as she rushed out of the pantry.

Her wish was short-lived.

Later on, their family buggy was barely out of the Koblenzes' driveway when Jane declared, "Why didn't you tell us Elden asked you to marry him?"

Millie found herself barely able to speak as her sisters congratulated her. By the time they were back in their own kitchen and their father was settled in his chair in the sitting room, her sisters were making plans for the wedding. Everyone was talking at once and Millie felt overwhelmed and a little shaky. They were all firing questions at her. Offering their opinions.

"Who will be your attendants?" Willa asked.

Beth chimed in, "Will you wait until next fall to marry since the season for weddings is past?"

"I see no reason to wait," Jane said. "That's old-fashioned. I think you should have a Christmas wedding."

"Christmas! That's less than three weeks away," Cora argued. "There isn't time to meet with the bishop and have the banns read before then."

"We need more time to get ready anyway," Henry said. "The house really needs to be painted if we're having a wedding here and…"

The sisters went on and on, but their voices faded as Millie tried to wrap her head around what had happened. Was there any way she and Elden could keep their betrothal a secret now? Between Jane and Willa, they'd soon spread the news through Honeycomb and beyond. Elden would have to tell his mother. It wouldn't be right for her to hear the news at Byler's deli counter.

Millie slipped out of the kitchen and into the hall, leaning against the wall for a moment and closing her eyes. She would have to go to Elden tomorrow and tell him what had happened.

Millie heard Eleanor's footsteps coming from the opposite end of the hall. No one could see her sister's prosthetic leg beneath her long skirts, but the rhythm of her gait was slightly different than others' and Millie recognized it at once.

"Hey," Eleanor said softly.

Millie pressed her lips together, feeling like she might cry but didn't know why. Elden wasn't going to be upset about others finding out the betrothal. He hadn't wanted to keep it a secret to begin with.

"Come on," Eleanor said gently as she looped her arm through Millie's. "Let's sit down." She led her into the parlor and indicated their mother's damask couch. "Relax a minute. I know you're excited, but I can see you're a bit overwhelmed, too."

Millie nodded, still not trusting herself to

speak, and sat down. Eleanor lit two oil lamps and then dropped onto the couch beside her. Although her sister was not physically demonstrative in the way their mother had been, Millie found Eleanor's nearness comforting.

"You didn't tell us," Eleanor said quietly. "Why not, *schweschter*?"

Her hands knotted together, Millie, turning teary, told Eleanor what had happened the day before, and Eleanor listened without interrupting.

When Millie was done, Eleanor was quiet for a moment, then said, "And why did you not want us to know?" She plucked a handkerchief from her sleeve and handed it to Millie. "Did you not think we'd be happy for you?"

Millie blotted her eyes and then her face. "It's not that I didn't want you to know. It was only that I…" She exhaled, her eyes feeling scratchy again. "I wanted to give him some more time. In case he wanted to change his mind," she managed. "Because why wouldn't he?"

"Oh, Millie," Eleanor whispered. "Why *would* he?"

"Because look at me." She gestured to her body miserably. "Why would a beautiful man like Elden want to be married to this?" She twisted the handkerchief in her hands. "Maybe I should go on a diet. Do you think I should go on a diet?"

Eleanor looked at her the way their mother had when one of them said something ridiculous. It was a kind disapproval without judgment. "You do not need to go on a diet," she said firmly. "You're healthy and this is how *Gott* made you, Millie. He also made you smart and capable and kind and such a hard worker. A woman with more faith I don't think I've ever known." She went quiet for a moment. "What's made you think you're not good enough for Elden, or that he doesn't really want this?"

Eleanor waited and when Millie didn't respond, she said, "Does this have something to do with his previous betrothal?"

Millie looked at her hands in her lap and shrugged. "I didn't really know Mary. I spoke to her a couple of times. I just know she's pretty and thin."

"Have you and Elden talked about her?"

Millie shrugged. "He's...um...mentioned her."

"Did he tell you why they broke up? Was it because of his mother?"

"I don't know," Millie admitted. "He doesn't like to talk about it."

Eleanor sat back on the couch. "That doesn't mean you don't have a right to know. I'm not saying you should talk about it all the time, or even ever again, but maybe you need to have a conversation about Mary. Once you know what happened, you'll feel more comfortable believing that Elden loves you and only you and he loves you as you are."

"I don't know if I can ask," Millie said miserably.

"I understand it will be hard, but you're going to be taking marriage vows. You need to know, Millie, so that you can be the wife you want to be to him. I think a few minutes of both of you being uncomfortable is worth it. I don't know a lot about marriage except what I saw between *Mam* and *Dat*, but I know there should never be secrets between husband and wife."

Millie knew Eleanor was right, but that didn't make it any easier. "Do you think we can ask the girls not to say anything for a few days? Until I can talk to Elden?"

"*Ya*, of course. I'll tell them now and be firm with them." Eleanor squeezed Millie's hand and stood. "And I won't pester you about this again. But believe me, you'll feel better once you talk to Elden. Once that's settled, you'll need to tell *Dat* about the betrothal and Elden should ask for your hand because *Dat* will like that. But you have my blessing, little sister." She smiled. "You deserve a husband like Elden. You need to believe that."

"*Ya,*" Millie whispered when her sister was gone. "I'm trying."

Elden tossed another bale of hay down from the barn loft and leaned over to speak to his uncle, who was standing below him on the ground floor. "You think that's enough? I can come back in a few days."

"Plenty." Gabriel waved his nephew down impatiently. "I told you and Elsie that I could do this myself, but nobody seems to want to listen to me. My wrist is just sprained, my hand hasn't been amputated."

"And the doctor told you to rest it, which means no heavy lifting." Elden came down the wire-wrung ladder attached to the wall. His uncle had sprained his wrist trying to lead a spooked yearling mare into the barn. "And that means bales of hay."

"You sound like Elsie now," Gabriel grumbled.

"You're a blessed man to have such a caring wife." Elden grabbed the two bales of hay, one in each gloved hand, and carried them to the aisle between the horse stalls where his uncle could easily get to it.

"That'll be you soon enough. I'm pleased for you, nephew. I'm glad to hear you're betrothed. From what I know of Millie, the two of you will make a fine couple."

Elden walked back and grabbed another two bales of hay. He agreed, of course, that Millie was perfect for him, though he worried she might change her mind. He fretted that he'd asked her too soon.

Millie had come over to his place the day after he proposed. He'd been cutting down pine and spruce trees to sell for Christmas trees. She'd told him that her sisters had accidentally found out about their betrothal and said it was only fair that he tell his mother and aunt and uncle. However, she asked him to hold off saying anything to anyone else yet. She'd agreed to go with him to Spence's Bazaar the following day to drop off the Christmas trees to be sold, but then she'd sent her sister over to cancel right before they were supposed to leave, saying she didn't feel well. He'd tried twice more to make a date with her, but they couldn't seem to make it happen. She was busy making Christmas items to sell at a booth she and her sisters had rented at Spence's Bazaar for an Amish Christmas market the following weekend. And it was a busy time of the year for him because of all his Christmas-related side businesses.

Elden kept telling himself there was no need to worry. They were both just busy. But he couldn't help but worry. Mary had avoided him before their breakup.

"I appreciate you agreeing I made the right choice of a wife," Elden said. "I wish *Mam* felt the same way."

"Pay no attention to Lavinia." Gabriel sat down on a bale of hay, cradling his sprained wrist that was wrapped in a stretchy bandage. "Your father used to say she'd complain about a sunny day. I think she's just worried that this is too soon after Mary."

"She wouldn't have thought it was too soon if it was Willa or Beth Koffman I'd proposed to. She was pushing hard this fall for me to court one of them."

Gabriel shrugged, watching him. "What can I say? Been married forty years and I still can't figure how women think."

Elden nodded and carried two more bales of hay to the growing stack in the center of the barn.

Both men were quiet, then Gabriel asked, "Is everything *oll recht* with you?"

"I'm *goot*." Elden flashed a smile.

"You don't seem *goot*. You seem worried. Newly betrothed to a girl like Millie, you ought to be a happy man."

"I am happy."

"You know, it's normal to be nervous." Gabriel pushed his wire-frame glasses up farther on his nose. "I asked Elsie to marry me and then I was petrified. Couldn't eat, couldn't sleep. I worried how we would make it financially. Where we would live. I fretted I wouldn't be the husband she deserved."

Elden walked back to where his uncle was sitting, but instead of grabbing another bale, he just stood there, listening to the howl of the wind outside. There was more snow in the forecast. "I love Millie, Gabriel. I'll be the happiest man in the county if she marries me."

"If?" Gabriel repeated. "I thought she said yes."

Elden stared at his boots. "*Ya*, she did. But so did Mary and we know how that worked out."

"Ah," Gabriel said. "Is that what this is about?" He paused thoughtfully, then said, "Millie is not Mary."

"I know that."

"Mary wasn't right for you. I told you that when you asked me. Your mother said the same thing."

Elden pulled off one leather work glove and drew his hand across his face. He was tired. He'd worked all day in the cold clearing. He needed a good night's sleep.

"It's only natural that you have this concern, but you need to dig deep and trust yourself. You've got to put those insecurities aside. *Gott* has brought you the right match and the past is the past. You have to believe that, *sohn*. You understand what I'm saying?"

Elden slid his hand back into his glove. "I do."

"Talk to Millie, that's my advice." Gabriel held up one hand, knotty with arthritis. "You didn't ask for it, but there it is, anyway. It's hard learning to discuss what you're feeling but I'm convinced it's one of the secrets to a good marriage. It took Elsie a long time to convince me of that, but, in the end, she was right." He stood and rested a comforting hand on Elden's shoulder. "It's going to be fine. You'll figure this out. You and Millie, together."

Elden nodded determinedly and prayed that his uncle was right.

Chapter Twelve

All the way home from Gabriel's, Elden thought about what his uncle had said about the necessity of believing in himself—and believing in himself and Millie as a couple. He knew he loved her, and not in the same way he had loved Mary. With Mary, he'd been so thrilled when she expressed interest in him that his feelings had quickly become almost a worship of her. Which he could see, looking back, had been wrong on more than one level. It wasn't an excuse, but he realized now that he'd been innocent of the love between a man and a woman. He'd gotten caught up in the thrill of the romance. He and Mary hadn't had that much in common. Not like he and Millie. Millie thought like he did and laughed at the same silly things. Millie was so easy to be with, and he liked who he was when he was with her.

Gabriel was right. Elden and Millie needed to talk. He wanted to tell her that her desire to keep their betrothal a secret made him fear she wasn't sure she wanted to marry him. He would admit to her that it brought back his insecurities concerning Mary, and even if that wasn't fair, it was how he felt. He needed to confess that he wasn't as confident a man as he appeared to be.

Gott must have been thinking the same thing, because as Elden approached his farm, he spotted Millie at the end of their driveway at the mailbox. She was as pretty as ever with a blue scarf over her head, and when she saw him, she gave him a smile that made him light-headed. Because her smile was for him alone.

He eased his buggy up next to her and slid open the window. "Need a ride?" he asked.

Samson wiggled his way under Elden's feet and set his front paws on the windowsill to greet her.

Millie laughed. Her cheeks rosy from the cold, she stroked the bulldog's head. There was a light dusting of snow on her scarf and a wisp of blond hair on her cheek that was damp. He ached to touch it.

"A ride where?" Millie asked. "I've only come to our mailbox to see if *Dat*'s copy of the *Budget* arrived. It should have been here yesterday and he's in a bad way."

"You don't even have a coat on," Elden pointed out.

She tugged at her sweater. "I didn't think I needed it for such a short trip." She looked up. "But then it started snowing again."

Samson gave a little bark as if he agreed.

"All right, boy. Off," Elden ordered, pointing at the floor. The dog obeyed, making his way to his favorite place on the passenger seat so he could look out the window.

"I could give you a ride back to your house," Elden told Millie.

She held the mail against her so it wouldn't get wet, laughing. "Elden, I don't need a ride."

"Oll recht." He grinned. "It's good to see you, Millie. I got so used to seeing you every day that missing a few days makes me feel... a bit lost," he said.

She took a step closer and rested one hand on the windowsill. "I've missed you, too, Elden."

When she said it, he knew it was true and silently chastised himself for questioning her feelings for him. Maybe he hadn't been able to read Mary, but he felt like he was finding his way with Millie. "When can I see you?" he asked. "We need to talk." He didn't think this was the best place to have the conversation they needed to have. Besides, he told himself, he wanted to plan what he was going to say. He went on quickly before he lost his nerve. "Look, Millie, I know I probably should have waited to ask you to marry me until we'd been courting longer. But it just came out. You looked so beautiful that day and I've known for some time that I wanted to spend my life with you and—" He looked away, fearful he would tear up. What would she think of him, a grown man crying?

Her hand was on the sill beside his and she brushed his fingertips with his. "*Ya*, we should talk." She exhaled. "Because either we're betrothed or we're not. It's not something to hide." Now she was the one who looked away.

"Don't worry," he whispered. "We'll figure this out. Because I do love you, Millie."

She lifted her lashes to look into his eyes. "And I love you, Elden," she murmured.

"You do?" His heart fluttered and he broke into a grin. She loved him!

"*Ya*, Elden. I've loved you my whole life, I think."

"Oh, Millie." Tying up the reins, he opened the buggy door and stepped down and pulled her into his arms because he didn't think he could live another moment without holding her. She fit perfectly against him, and they stood in the falling snow with her head on his chest, her armful of mail between them.

"This is nice," she murmured.

Elden was too full of emotion to speak, so he just held her.

She was the one who came to her senses first. She gave a bubbly laugh and stepped back. "Enough of that." She looked up at him shyly. "If your mother or my father sees us, we'll both be in hot water."

"Ya." He couldn't stop smiling, because everything really was going to be all right. Just as Gabriel had said. "When can I see you?"

"Ach." She wiped at her face, which was wet from the snow. "We've so many projects to finish up before the Amish Christmas market on Saturday. And Jane and Beth have both caught terrible colds, so we're not getting our items to sell ready as quickly as we thought. Will you be there?"

"Ya, I'm selling my fresh-cut Christmas trees and some of the wreath frames. Might make some wreaths if I have time. I reserved

an outside booth. You know, because of the trees." He slid his hands in his pockets, mostly so he wouldn't be tempted to hug her again. "I don't know if I'll be able to see you until it's over. JJ was going to help me but now he can't."

"We rented a table inside." She looked up at him. "We could do something after. I could ride there with my family and then you and I could go somewhere afterward."

"Good idea." He raised his eyebrows. "I think it's over at three. We could go out for an early supper. We've never eaten out together and we'll already be in town. There's this mint milkshake that's only available this time of year at one of the fast-food places. Want to go?"

Her eyes lit up. "I love mint milkshakes!" Then she grimaced. "Oh, but what about your mother? If she's going to the market? If you have to take her home first, I should go home with my family and we can leave from there."

"She may be going, I'm not sure. Knowing her, she won't want to miss it." He chuckled. "But I'll have someone else take her home. Don't worry about it." He looked into her eyes again and wished he could stand there forever with her. But she wasn't dressed for the snow in her thin sweater, and she was getting wet. "You should go in. You sure you don't want a ride?"

"No ride, Elden. I've two feet." She ran her hand down his coat sleeve. "I'll see you Saturday. *Ya?*"

"Saturday," he agreed and got into his buggy. But he didn't back out of her driveway right away. Instead, he sat there watching Millie walk up her lane, imagining what it would be like when her lane was his—*theirs*—and then when he walked in the door at the end of each day, she would be waiting for him.

By noon Saturday, the Amish Christmas market was packed. Spence's Bazaar had rented out every available space inside the sprawling building as well as outside in a parking lot. Amish men and women were selling baked and canned goods, quilts, wooden toys and greenery. *Englishers* had also rented space and were selling all sorts of holiday frippery that was definitely not Plain. There were Christmas tree ornaments that flashed red, white and blue, plastic dolls in red velvet skirts, sweaters one could have their dog's name embroidered on while they waited, and so many Christmas stockings that it made Millie's head spin. There was Christmas music playing loudly from speakers and so many *Englishers* with their big voices that it was overwhelming.

Millie and her sisters were having a good sales day, which made up for all the chaos around them. Each of them had contributed in some way. They sold knitted hats, scarves and mittens, potpourri sachets from dry pine needles and jars of jam with pretty scraps of fabric and ribbons on the tops. Then they had baked goods: dozens of Christmas cookies as well as apple tarts and pecan sticky buns they'd made with the nuts they'd picked from their own trees.

At first it was fun, but as the day wore on, the Koffman sisters all began to look forward to returning home to their quieter, simpler lives. And Millie was looking forward to her date with Elden. A date with her betrothed. She had to keep reminding herself of that. She was engaged to be married. Unfortunately, she'd been so busy that she hadn't had a chance to go outside to say hello to Elden. It seemed like their line of customers never got any shorter, and without Jane and Beth, home sick, they worked nonstop selling their goods.

It wasn't until a few minutes before the market officially closed that Millie was finally able to catch her breath. She sat down on a metal chair and had a long drink of water. "My feet are so tired," she muttered, wishing now that she'd worn her leather shoes that were sturdier than the sneakers she'd chosen. "I almost wish I hadn't told Elden I'd go out with him tonight."

"Want me to go out with him instead?" Willa teased.

Millie laughed. "I think not."

"Are you leaving straight from here?" Eleanor tucked a handful of cash she'd counted into a tin box.

"I think so, but I'm not sure." Millie took another sip of water and fished a piece of gingerbread cookie from a bag of broken ones they'd brought along for snacking. The crowds had thinned out so that few shoppers were passing their table now. "I haven't gotten to talk to him yet. I saw him when I went to get our sandwiches and we waved to each other, but he was busy trimming branches off a tree for a woman carrying a dog in her pocketbook."

"I saw Lavinia earlier," Henry said. She was busy stacking empty wooden crates to take home. They'd sold nearly every single item they'd brought with them. The only items left were a few jars of pickled beets, a loaf of country white bread and a few bags of cookies. "She said something about going to the fabric store with Elsie and then home. I guess that means she's catching a ride with Gabriel."

"Why don't you go see what your plans are, Millie?" Eleanor suggested, counting another stack of money. There was relief all over their big sister's face. They had made a lot of money today.

"You sure?" Millie asked. "You don't want me to help clean up?"

"Not much to clean up, is there?" Cora looked up from a paperback book on local plants that she'd bought from a stall nearby. "We sold most everything."

The Christmas music that had been blasting for hours stopped suddenly in the middle of a song and they all seemed to sigh in unison. It felt like the sixth or seventh time they'd heard the song about a grandmother being trampled by a reindeer.

"Go on, Millie," Eleanor encouraged. "Let us know what you're doing once you know." She glanced around. "It won't take us long to finish up here. If we're not here when you return, we'll be at the buggy."

Millie snugged her black bonnet over her organza *kapp* and reached for her cloak in the pile behind them. The building that was little more than a pole shed had been warm enough when it was packed with people, but it was cool now. "Be right back," she said. She'd been so busy all day that she hadn't had time to think about her date, but now she could feel her excitement bubbling inside her.

He had mentioned the other day when they saw each other that they needed to talk. She imagined he meant about when they were going to tell others they were engaged, and she had decided she was going to tell him she was ready now. And maybe this would be a good time to ask him about his breakup with Mary. And to talk about when they should make an appointment to speak with their bishops. There was also the matter of when they wanted to marry. It wasn't the Amish way to have long courtships, but she wanted to know what he was thinking.

Millie tied her cloak as she walked away from the table, her gaze settling on an Amish woman she didn't know, cuddling a baby on her shoulder. The infant's head rested against its mother and Millie wondered what it would feel like to have her own baby. To have Elden's baby. The thought was scary, but it made her heart ache in an unfamiliar way.

Passing the woman with her child, Millie wove her way through the building where everyone else was breaking down their makeshift shops. She passed through one of the exit doors and crossed the paved parking lot toward where Elden was set up. She could see that every one of his trees was gone and the only thing left was a freestanding post he'd used to hang wreaths on.

As she walked, her eyes scanned for him and then she saw him, his back to her. She'd know him anywhere: his slender build, broad shoulders and blond hair sticking out from beneath his beanie. As she drew closer, she saw him gesturing and realized he was talking to someone. She was just about to call out to him when he moved and she recognized who it was.

Her breath was knocked from her and she froze. *It couldn't be.* Tears filled her eyes.

It was Mary. His betrothed. And even from this distance, she could hear Elden laughing. She saw him smiling down at the woman: the petite, beautiful Mary with her honey-colored hair and hazel eyes. And Mary was smiling at him the way a woman smiled at her beau. The way Millie smiled at him.

For a very brief time, Millie had thought Elden might really marry her. But, in her heart of hearts, she had known it would never happen. She had known that day when she had fallen over the fence that no matter how much she loved him, he would never be hers. She had known that men so perfect, so beautiful inside and out, didn't marry girls like her. They married perfect girls like Mary.

Millie found it difficult to catch her breath. She closed her eyes, fearing she might faint, and she hung her head, taking in great gulps of cold air.

Mary had returned for Elden.

And there he was smiling at her. Welcoming her home.

What did Millie do now? Did she walk away? She certainly wasn't going to make a scene. She cared too much for Elden to do that. And what would be the point, other than everyone talking later about how foolish Millie Koffman had been about a man who could never have been hers.

Nay, she was better than that. But she couldn't just walk away, either.

Millie took a deep, shuddering breath and forced herself to put one foot in front of the other. She walked right over to Mary and Elden, and without looking at him, she smiled at Mary and her perfect teeth and her perfect slender little face and said, "Mary, I didn't know you were back. Millie Koffman," she introduced herself.

"Good to see you again," Mary said in a melodic voice. Her eyes, however, suggested that she was trying to place Millie. She didn't seem to remember her, even though she'd lived within miles of Millie for almost a year. Of course that was because skinny girls like Mary didn't remember fat girls like Millie.

"Visiting for long?" Millie asked, afraid her face would crack from her smile.

"I—" Mary looked at Elden. "I'm not sure."

Millie turned toward Elden but didn't look at him because she couldn't bear it. "Could I speak to you?" she asked, not recognizing her own voice. This had to be one of the hardest things she had ever done in her life. As hard, as terrible, as saying goodbye to her mother.

Before Elden could respond, Millie walked to the edge of the parking lot, the wet snow slushy at her feet. The horses and cars and foot traffic had made a muck of the pristine snow and now it was soiled with dirt and manure and discarded candy wrappers and soda pop cans.

Her back was to him when he approached.

"What's wrong?"

He reached out to touch her shoulder as he

walked around to face her and she pulled away. She couldn't let him touch her because if he did, surely she would shatter. And then no one would be able to pick up the pieces, not even her family who loved her.

"I release you," she said, her voice so soft that he leaned closer.

"What did you say?"

Still, she couldn't look at him. Instead, she focused on a greasy bit of snow on the toe of her boot. "I release you," she said louder. "From our betrothal agreement."

"You what?" he asked.

"I won't marry you," she said. "I… I don't want to marry you, Elden."

He just stood there, his arms at his side, and said nothing.

What was there to say?

Millie made it all the way to her buggy before she burst into tears.

Chapter Thirteen

Millie sat at the kitchen table and stared out the windows at the falling rain. The cold front that had brought the unexpected snow Thanksgiving week and continued through early December had finally passed and the temperatures had warmed up some.

She sighed and spun her ceramic mug between her hands. The peppermint tea Beth had made her had cooled, but she didn't want it anyway. The kitchen was warm with the scent of cinnamon rolls baking in the oven. At the counter, Jane was busy whipping up an orange cream cheese frosting for the top of the rolls. She'd made a batch of the frosting to try, adding orange zest to the recipe. She planned to prepare more rolls the following day to be popped into the oven Christmas morning.

By the time their family finished their morning devotionals, which would include reading the entire Christmas story from the Bible, the rolls would be ready to come out of the oven. Their mother's orange cinnamon rolls had been a Christmas tradition for as long as Millie could remember, and ordinarily, she would have been excited about the special treat. But since the day of the Christmas market, she hadn't been able to get excited about anything. That included her and Annie's annual tradition of making Christmas cards together to go along with the cookies, cakes and other treats their families would deliver on Christmas Eve. Millie was now waiting for her friend to arrive.

Continuing to stare out the window at the rivulets of rain on the glass, she listened to Jane humming a Christmas hymn as she worked. She wished she'd canceled with Annie. She wasn't in the mood for making Christmas cards. She wasn't in the mood to do anything but lie in her bed and cry, except that after ten days of crying she'd run out of tears. Now all she did was sit dry-eyed and stare, much the same way she had after their mother passed. This somehow felt worse, and she didn't know why. Maybe because her mother had gone to heaven and Elden was here in Honeycomb, in the arms of his girlfriend.

Millie lowered her head to her hands on the table. If Jane noticed, she didn't say anything, likely because she was afraid to. All her sisters tiptoed around Millie, whispering to each other, making her feel invisible. Which was okay with her because she wished she could just disappear. She hurt so badly that the pain was physical. She had so many feelings and confused thoughts in her head that it was hard sometimes for her to breathe.

The first couple of days after Millie broke up with Elden, her sisters had tried to be helpful. They had attempted to talk to her, to make her things she liked to eat. They had even offered to do her chores so she could rest. They insisted over and over that Elden would come to her as soon as he came to his senses, that what Millie had seen with him and Mary had all been a misunderstanding.

Millie hadn't expected Elden to come to her after their breakup because there had been no misunderstanding. Mary had come back to him. The hows and whys didn't matter and there was no need for Millie to continue to analyze the situation.

Of course, she couldn't help herself. All she

did was think about Elden and why he had chosen Mary over her. She even tried to place the blame elsewhere. She wondered if Lavinia had brought Mary back to Honeycomb. Maybe Lavinia had written to Mary and asked her to return to Honeycomb because she preferred her son marry her than Millie.

But what did it matter how it had happened? Elden was with Mary now. Of course a tiny part of her hoped he might come and tell her how she'd misread what she'd seen between him and Mary that day. But he hadn't come by in ten days' time, which was proof that she hadn't misunderstood anything.

Initially after the breakup, Millie's sisters thought that the relationship could still be mended. But Elden hadn't sought Millie out and Willa had heard that Mary was back in Honeycomb to stay. Then her sisters had changed their approach. They'd suggested Millie should go to him. For closure, they said. Eleanor had sat on the edge of Millie's bed one night, something she had never done in her life, and talked to her in the dark. Her oldest sister advised Millie to speak with Elden so that she could move on. So he could move on and know there were no hard feelings. Eleanor had said that no matter how painful it would be to speak to him about what had happened with Mary, talking with him would allow Millie to emotionally set Elden aside and prepare herself for the husband *Gott* had planned for her.

But Millie couldn't do it. Even though what Eleanor said made sense, Millie couldn't bring herself to confront Elden. She had all sorts of justifications, like it would only make her feel worse or he wouldn't want to speak to her anyway. And when her thoughts turned ugly, she told herself she certainly wasn't going to go to make him feel better for returning to Mary. Why did he deserve to feel better when she was in the depths of despair?

The moment ugly thoughts like those crossed her mind, Millie squeezed her eyes shut and prayed to *Gott* to take such darkness from her heart. She didn't want to be that woman. She didn't want to be a self-centered, spiteful fat girl. She just wanted to be herself again. She feared, however, that she never again would be the hopeful woman she once was.

The sound of buggy wheels caught Millie's attention and she glanced out the window.

"Looks like Annie is here," Jane said cheerfully. "Cora and Beth set everything up in the parlor on a card table for you. Cora got you some new glue and some glitter that looks like snow. And there's lots of card stock and old Christmas cards that you can cut up to make your new cards." She returned to her frosting, then spun back around to Millie. "Could you make one for Aunt Judy and Uncle Cyrus? I'm going to give them some of these rolls. So they can have something special for Christmas morning, too."

"*Ya*, we can make a card for them," Millie said without much enthusiasm. Through the window, she watched Henry come out of the barn in a rain slicker and grab the halter of Annie's horse. Once Annie was hurrying toward the door with a big basket on her arm, Henry led the horse and buggy into the barn.

There was a rap on the mudroom door and Annie let herself in. Millie's mother had often referred to Annie as her eighth daughter. When *Mam* had been in a teasing mood, she'd refer to Annie as her *favorite* daughter.

"*Hallo!*" Annie sang.

"*Ya*, in the kitchen." Millie didn't rise from her chair. She heard the rustle of Annie's coat, and her friend walked into the room.

"*Hallo*, Jane!"

"*Goot* afternoon, Annie." Jane glanced Millie's way. "Glad you're here. We all are. Millie could use some cheering up."

She was about to tell Jane that she was sorry that her heartbreak was inconveniencing others within the household, but she held her tongue. A few months ago, their preacher had talked about the evil in the world and that parishioners needed to be vigilant to recognize it. Such mean thoughts made Millie fear the devil was too close to her for comfort. Because what if he was the one putting those unkind thoughts in her head?

"I brought some more old greeting cards." Annie set down her basket. "And new envelopes. And *Mam* sent some markers in green and red and silver and gold. She bought them especially for us."

Millie slowly rose from her chair. "That was nice of her," she said, trying to sound enthusiastic.

Annie turned to her, searching her gaze. "How are you?"

Millie's lowered lip quivered and she bit down on it.

"Oh, Millie." Annie threw her arms around her friend in a generous hug. "I am so sorry. You still haven't talked to him?"

Millie shook her head. "He doesn't want to talk to me. If he did, he'd have come by now."

Annie stepped back, her brow furrowing.

"You want me to go over there right now and give him a piece of my mind? Because I will. You know I will. I can't stand that he's hurt you this way."

Millie shook her head, her gaze falling to the hardwood floor between them. "What would be the sense in talking? Now that Mary's back—" She didn't finish her sentence.

"And they're definitely courting again?" Annie's gaze flitted to Jane, who was all ears. "Jane?"

"I've heard talk," Millie's little sister said, her gaze moving to Millie, then back to Annie. "But nobody knows what's going on. I do know that Mary and Elden haven't been seen out together."

"Of course not. He's not a bad person," Millie said softly. "He would keep it quiet, at least for a little while." She felt tears sting the backs of her eyelids. "He's not trying to hurt me. He's not like that."

Annie gritted her teeth. "I'll tell you one thing. I'd like to hurt him right now." She raised a pudgy fist.

Something close to a laugh burst out of Millie. She grabbed Annie's hand and lowered it to the girl's side. "Annie, we don't hit people. That's not who we are."

Annie exhaled, flexing her fingers. "I know. I didn't say I was *going* to do it. Only that I wanted to." Her tone softened. "Do you still want to make the cards, or do you not feel like it?" Her eyes filled with concern. "We don't have to do it this year if you don't want to. I'll stay and visit with you, but we don't have to do anything."

Millie stood there for a moment in indecision. She didn't feel like making the cards, but if she didn't, what was she going to do but sit around and mope? Maybe keeping her hands busy would keep her mind active and off Elden. She forced a half smile. "*Nay.* Let's do them. Come on." She headed out of the kitchen. "Beth and Cora were nice enough to get us all set up in the parlor."

"I'll bring a plate of cookies in and some hot chocolate," Jane called after them.

Her words made Millie's heavy heart a little lighter. It was true she had lost Elden, and she knew, no matter what anyone said, she would never love another man. But Jane and Annie reminded her of how blessed she was to have so many others to love and be loved by. And she'd just have to be content with that.

Elden rested on his back, his head under the kitchen sink, and tightened the connection on the new drainpipe he'd installed. "Could you turn the water on, *Mam*?" he asked, his voice strange in his ears. It sounded so heavy. "To be sure there's no leak."

His mother, who had been hovering over him the entire time he was making the repair, turned on the faucet, and he heard water running down the drain. He studied the new PVC pipe at the connections and deeming it didn't leak, slid out from under the sink. Rolling onto his hands and knees, he gathered his tools and the damp towel he'd used to mop up any excess water. "Good as new," he proclaimed, standing.

"*Ach*, I can't believe I was so foolish to push the compost bucket against the pipe and crack it. *Danki, sohn*. What would I do without you? Now I can make a proper Christmas Eve supper."

He returned the plumber's glue and tools to his toolbox on the counter and handed her the wet towel. "No need to cook. I'm not that hungry. We can have the leftover brats and sauerkraut from yesterday." When she didn't respond, he turned to look at her.

She'd thrown the towel over a chair and was standing behind him, arms crossed over her chest the way she had when he was a little boy and she was displeased with him. "You have to eat. You haven't eaten well since—" She stopped and started again. "I'd say it's time you saw the doctor, but I don't think he can fix what ails you."

Elden held up his hand. "Please, *Mam*. Let's not start this again. What's done is done. I'm fine." He turned from the counter, his toolbox in his hand, thinking he would return it to his workshop where he could be alone and stay there until supper.

But his mother blocked his way. "*Nay*, you're not fine, Elden. I've never seen you in a state like this. Not even after the business with Mary."

He closed his eyes for a moment, praying for patience. He opened his eyes. "Please let's not talk about this."

"We *are* going to talk about it because I'm tired of watching you mope about."

Realizing he wasn't going to be able to get away from her, he set his toolbox down hard on the counter. "I'm *not* moping," he argued, an edge to his voice.

Of course she was right; he was moping. All he did was mope. His heart was broken. Millie Koffman had broken his heart. The interesting thing about it was that he had believed that Mary had broken his heart, only to learn now that what he had experienced after that breakup was a bruised heart. The difference was vast. Without Millie, he felt lost, unmoored, and a shell of himself. Only now, in a depth of pain that he felt physically, did he understand what it meant to truly love a woman. And lose her.

"It's time you did something," his mother went on. "I don't care what you do but do something. Go talk to Millie and find out if this can be mended. The fact that you refuse to even talk to her is beyond my understanding," she fumed. "I always thought you were a bright boy, but now, I admit I may have overestimated you."

Her words almost made him laugh. This was supposed to make him feel better? "I thought you'd be happy we broke up."

"Why would I be happy?" she asked incredulously. "You're miserable. No mother wants her son to be unhappy."

"But you didn't like Millie. Not from that day we had that first supper with the Koffmans."

She planted both hands on her hips. "When did I say I didn't like Millie? I never said I didn't like Millie. She's a sweet girl."

Elden squared off with her, imitating her

stance with his arms crossed over his chest. "Come to think of it, you didn't like Mary, either."

Lavinia pointed at him. "Now, *that*'s true. I didn't like Mary, at least not for you. She's a shallow, selfish girl. And she makes a terrible *hassenpfeffer*."

He laughed without humor. "You'd judge a woman's character by how well she cooks rabbit? You don't even like *hassenpfeffer*."

"We're not talking about rabbit," she quipped. "We're talking about you. You need to speak to that girl. You didn't even tell me why she broke up with you. Did you have a fight? You know quarrels are just part of two people getting to know each other. And don't think that after you're married there won't be disagreements. Your father and I never had a cross word between us until after we were married. And you of all people knew we could disagree, but we loved and respected each other."

"Millie and I didn't have a fight."

She shook her head so hard that the strings of her kapp *whipped* about. "You didn't have a fight? Then why did she break up with you?"

"I don't know," he blurted. Emotion rose in Elden's throat and he looked away.

"You don't know?" she repeated. "What do

you mean you don't know? That's ridiculous. It's been nearly two weeks and you haven't bothered to march over there and ask her why?"

It wasn't that Elden had no idea. He suspected that it had something to do with Mary stopping to speak with him at the Christmas market. She'd just returned to Honeycomb to spend Christmas with her cousins and she had wanted to say hello. He had gotten the feeling that she wanted to broach the subject of them dating again, but when he told her he was betrothed, she'd seemed genuinely happy for him. That hadn't stopped her from flirting with him, but that was just how Mary was. She flirted with everyone.

The thing was, Millie hadn't asked him why Mary was there. It was a misunderstanding that could have been easily set right. But what would have been the point? The next time she thought he'd done something wrong, she'd break up with him again. And what if he did actually do something wrong, which was bound to happen at some point. After all, he was human, with human failings. He was going to make mistakes in their relationship no matter how much he loved her.

But maybe his failings were too great, he had decided. Mary had broken up with him.

Millie had broken up with him. Maybe he wasn't the kind of man women wanted to marry. Maybe it was best he accept being a bachelor and focus on caring for his mother and the farm his father had left him.

"Elden? Elden! Are you listening to a word I say?" his mother asked.

Elden blinked. He hadn't been listening.

"I'm telling you, you need to go speak to Millie. I imagine she's as miserable as you are. Maybe she's changed her mind and doesn't know how to tell you that she made a terrible mistake. And if she hasn't changed her mind, at least you'll know that." She threw up her hand. "Then you can move on. And stop this moping."

"I am not moping." Elden emphasized each word. "And I'm not going to the Koffmans'."

"Fine!" His mother threw her arms up in the air in surrender, turned around and walked away.

"*Fine*," he repeated. He picked up his toolbox again. "While I have my plumbing tools, I may as well check that faucet in the upstairs bathroom." He watched her march out of the kitchen and into the laundry room, where she grabbed her wool cloak. "Where are you going?" he asked.

She threw on her cloak and began to tie it beneath her chin, her motions jerky.

"You're not going to the Koffmans', are you?" he asked, suddenly feeling panicky. "*Mutter*, you can't go there."

"I'm going to Trudy's," she said sternly. She marched back into the kitchen and scooped up a plate of rice cereal treats she'd decorated with white chocolate and red and green sprinkles and dropped it into a basket.

"It's going to get dark before you make it home," he called after her as she strode out of the kitchen again. Her friend Trudy lived on the property behind them, but there was an old logging road they used to pass between the two farms. "Take a flashlight!"

In response, she slammed the back door on her way out.

Chapter Fourteen

Late afternoon on Christmas Eve, Millie sat at the kitchen table with her *dat*, a checkerboard between them. Behind them, Eleanor was tidying up the counter and putting away clean dishes. Millie rested her elbow on the table, her chin in her hand, as she watched him contemplate his next move. Or was he daydreaming, she wondered. He stared at the board, but his eyes were unfocused.

Millie glanced at the wall clock, which seemed to have been ticking in slow motion all day. In another hour, it would be time to begin preparing their supper. She glanced out the big windows that looked out over the barnyard. The rain had ended that morning, and according to Henry, the temperature had dropped. Jane wanted snow for Christmas Day even though it wasn't in the forecast.

Millie's attention returned to her father. "*Dat*," she said gently. "It's your move."

He pushed his round, wire-frame glasses higher on his nose and looked at her. He'd aged five years since their mother had died. She wondered if her father's confusion was caused by the loss of his beloved wife, or because of the dementia. Either way, it was sad.

"You know that I know your mother's dead, right?" he said.

His comment surprised her. "*Ya*," she murmured, not sure she believed him. "I know."

"I just like to pretend she isn't sometimes." He sighed. "She always loved Christmas. She loved everything about it—the baking, the sewing, the visiting and the celebration of Christ's birth." He worked his jaw. "She especially loved those orange cinnamon rolls she always made for Christmas morning."

Millie covered his veined, thin hand with hers. "Jane made the rolls. We'll still have them tomorrow morning after our devotions."

He smiled tenderly, his eyes rheumy. "*Goot.* That would make my Aggie happy." He hesitated and then went on. "You know she wants her girls to be happy. She wants all of us to be happy. I try to remind myself of that when I miss her too much."

Millie couldn't help but smile as she stared at the checkerboard. "I know, *Dat*," she said, patting his hand.

"Uh-oh," he responded, his tone suddenly childish.

She looked up at him, wondering what had brought on the change. "What is it?"

"A storm blowing in."

"What?" she said, glancing out the window, then back at him. The sky was gray and cloudless, but the trees were barely bending in the breeze. "I don't think it's going to storm."

"Oh, it's going to be a storm all right. See the look on her face?" He pointed.

"What are you talking about, *Dat*?" Millie looked out the window again.

Then she saw her. A tall, thick woman in a black cloak and black bonnet striding determinedly toward the back door, a basket on her elbow. Lavinia.

Millie came out of her chair, almost knocking it over. "Ellie!" she breathed. She could barely find her voice. "It's Lavinia." She made for the hall, not even taking the time to push in her chair.

"Lavinia?" Eleanor dried her hands on a dish towel. "What's she doing here on Christmas Eve?"

"Maybe come to play checkers," their father suggested, which in any other circumstances might have made them laugh.

"She didn't come to play checkers, *Dat*." Eleanor looked to Millie, who was nearly out of the kitchen. "Where are you going?"

"I don't know. But I don't want to hear what she has to say." Millie covered her ears with her hands, panic fluttering in her chest. "I don't want to hear about Elden and Mary. She's probably here to announce their betrothal."

"Oh, Millie, stop. She wouldn't come here to tell us Elden—"

A loud rap at the back door drowned out Eleanor's last words. The knock was immediately followed by a series of bangs. "*Hallo! Hallo*, it's Lavinia! Can I come in? Coming in!" she hollered and the back door opened.

"I'm not here!" Millie whispered harshly and ran down the hallway.

"Lavinia! What a surprise," Millie heard Eleanor greet from the kitchen. "Come in and warm yourself."

When she reached the parlor door, Millie ducked in. But then, her curiosity got the better of her, and she hid out of sight, eavesdropping.

"I brought these for you, Felty. They're the ones with the sprinkles on top," Lavinia shouted. "The kind you told me you like." She was speaking louder than necessary, something Millie had noticed Lavinia had been doing frequently with her father. As if he would understand better if she said things louder. The funny thing was that his hearing was better than Lavinia's.

"Ah, more rice cereal bars," Eleanor said. "How nice. We'll have them after supper tonight."

"I'm having one now," their father announced.

"Let me take your cloak, Lavinia. Would you like a cup of tea? Coffee?"

Millie heard Lavinia removing her coat and handing it to Eleanor.

"I think I would like tea. And maybe a little snack? I know Jane's got cookies or something around here. I was expecting a nice big tin of homemade Christmas cookies from you and then my son mucked things up, didn't he?"

What was she talking about, Millie wondered. What had Elden said to her? Did Lavinia think Elden was the one who had broken up with her? The remarkable thing was that her words suggested she was *not* pleased with the breakup.

A chair scraped and Millie heard Lavinia

drop heavily into it. "I've come to talk to you about Millie, Eleanor. It's time someone with a little sense butted into this mess. I think you and I both have sense, don't you?"

"*Goot*," Millie's father said, his mouth full. "Having another."

Millie heard Eleanor walk into the mud-room, then back into the kitchen. "I'm sorry, Lavinia, but I can't talk about Millie behind her back," she said carefully. "This sounds like you need to talk to her."

"Fine," Lavinia huffed. "Millie? Where are you?" she called loudly. "I know very well you're here! I saw you from the window, running to get away from me!"

Millie felt her cheeks grow hot, and she squeezed her eyes shut, embarrassed the widow had caught her.

"Why don't I find Millie?" Eleanor said.

"Or just call her to get in here. You know she's hiding in the back of the house."

Millie considered trying to sneak upstairs, but before she could make a dash for the steps, she heard Eleanor's unmistakable gait.

"Millie?" Eleanor called in a whisper.

Millie stepped into the hall, staring at her big sister, round-eyed.

"I suppose you heard all that." Eleanor

stopped in front of Millie. "I don't know what's going on or what she wants from us, but I think you should talk to her."

Millie's gazed flitted toward the kitchen, then back to her sister. "I'm afraid of what she might say."

"So afraid that you won't talk to her, even if there's a chance," Eleanor whispered, "that you might be able to get Elden back?"

"I don't want him now, not after he's gone back to Mary," Millie hissed back.

"*Ach*, I see." Eleanor met her gaze with a hard stare. "How did *Mam* put it? You're willing to cut off your nose to spite your face?"

Millie hung her head and they were both quiet for a moment. She could hear Lavinia talking in the kitchen.

"Don't eat them all, Felty!" Lavinia told him. "There will be none for anyone else. Give me one."

Millie met Eleanor's gaze. "Do you think there's a chance?" she asked, her heart pounding.

"I don't know, but I think it's worth hearing what his mother has to say. Don't you?"

Millie nodded and Eleanor gave her a big hug. "Come on," Eleanor said. "Lavinia's the one who ought to be scared. Taking on the Koffman girls."

A smile came unexpectedly to Millie and she followed her big sister down the hall.

"There you are, Millie," Lavinia declared, munching on a rice cereal bar. "I thought I was going to have to play hide-and-seek with you. Sit down."

She pulled out a chair beside her and Millie felt as if she had no choice but to sit.

"I'll make tea for all of us," Eleanor offered.

"I want hot chocolate," their father declared. "With marshmallows. And don't skimp. It's Christmas Eve."

"I'm not going to futz about with you, Millie." Lavinia took a napkin from a basket on the table and wiped the sticky crumbs from her mouth. "I'm here because that ridiculous son of mine won't come." She pursed her lips. "Why did you break up with him?"

Millie was so surprised by the abrupt question that it took her a moment to respond. But, if Lavinia could be so curt, why couldn't she? "Because Mary came back to him. I saw them together and they were laughing, and it was obvious she was still in love with him."

Lavinia rolled her eyes. "The two of you belong together. Neither of you have any sense. You know she was the one who broke up with him, right? Said he wasn't good enough for her. Thought she could do better."

Millie blinked in disbelief. "I… I thought… People said you broke them up. That you didn't think she was good enough for him."

"Second part was true. She wasn't. Isn't." Lavinia waved in dismissal. "A smart girl like you, you'd think you'd have enough sense not to listen to gossip. It's rarely accurate. Though I wasn't surprised when I heard people thought I was the one responsible."

Millie's brow furrowed. "You knew people were saying you broke them up? And you didn't correct them?"

"And what? Tell people that *she* broke up with him? I knew how much he was struggling with the rejection. Why make it worse by telling people it was her and not me?" She shrugged. "What do I care what people say about me? I know the truth." She pointed heavenward. "And *Gott* knows." She met Millie's gaze. "But none of that matters. What matters is you talking some sense into my boy."

Millie's respect for Lavinia had increased tenfold in a matter of seconds. Elden had insisted his mother had a good heart, and now Millie saw it. But she still didn't understand Lavinia. "I'm confused," she said. "I thought you didn't want him to marry me. You're always watching me, criticizing me."

Lavinia snorted. "This isn't about me, but if you want to marry Elden, you best get used to my ways. I don't mean anything by my words. I just say what I'm thinking at the moment." She put her hand on Millie's. "I like you. And more importantly, you like my son. *Nay*. You love him. That Mary Yost, she never loved him. Only person she loves is herself."

Their father reached into the basket of treats and Lavinia pulled it away before he could grab another. "I told you that's enough, Felty." She looked back at Millie. "You misunderstood what you saw that day at the market. Maybe Mary did return from Kentucky hoping to find her way back to my Elden, but he only had eyes for you by then. We've not seen hide nor hair of her since the Christmas market."

Millie stared at the older woman. "You haven't?"

"*Nay*, and since you broke up with Elden, all he's done is mope around the house. Barely speaks, barely eats. Not even that dog of his can cheer him up." Lavinia sat back in her chair. "I think my son's too afraid to talk to you. And that's on me, I suppose. I should have raised him better. His father always said

I spoiled him. And maybe I did." She crossed her arms. "So, what do you say? Will you at least talk to him so he knows what happened?"

Millie's heart was beating so hard in her chest that she could barely hear herself think.

"Well?" Lavinia demanded.

Millie looked at Eleanor, who was leaning against the counter. She could tell by the look on her big sister's face what she was thinking.

Before she lost her nerve, Millie got to her feet.

"That'a girl," Lavinia said. "You make this right and you and I will make a good pair. We'll handle him. He has a soft heart. He's a hard worker. But he's still a man." She pulled the basket toward her and took out two treats, handing one to Millie's father. "Practically gone now, Felty. You may as well have another."

Trembling, Millie walked over to Eleanor. All she could think of was what a terrible mistake she had made. How could she have done such a thing to Elden, to have judged him without even asking him what had taken place with Mary? Her decision, she realized, had been about herself and not him, not them. How could she have thought so little of herself as to have assumed he didn't want her?

"What are you standing there, for?" Eleanor asked, the slightest hint of a smile on her face. "Go talk to him. Lavinia will stay here with me to give you two some privacy." She looked over Millie's shoulder. "Won't you, Lavinia?" Her tone was firm.

"No need for me to go." Lavinia munched on her treat. "Already been down that road. He won't listen to me."

Eleanor grasped Millie's hands and looked into her eyes, smiling. "Talk to him," she said softly. "If your love is true, and I think it is, together you can find a way through this."

Millie whipped around, practically running for the mudroom. Behind her, she heard her father get out of his chair and a moment later, he was beside her, taking his barn coat from a peg.

"*Dat*, where are you going?"

"With you. To talk some sense into that boy."

Millie pulled on her cloak. "*Dat*, you stay here. Ellie!" she called. "Tell *Dat* he has to stay here."

Eleanor came to the doorway. *"Dat—"*

"It doesn't matter if I forget to brush my teeth sometimes," he interrupted, stepping into his boots as he slipped into his coat. "I'm still the father. And I'm still the head of this household, and I'm going."

Millie started to protest and then gave in. So what if her father went? All she wanted to do was to get to Elden now. To apologize. To tell him how sorry she was that she had made such a muck of things. "Fine." She pulled on her boots.

"Millie, if—" Eleanor said.

"*Nay*, it's all right if he comes. He can't make a bigger mess of this than I have."

Grinning, Millie's father followed her down the porch steps and ten minutes later, they walked into Elden's barnyard.

The bulldog spotted them from the barn door that was half-open and barked and raced toward them. "There's my boy! That's my good dog," *Dat* said, rushing to greet Samson.

Elden walked out of the barn. Seeing Millie, he halted, his arms hanging at his sides. He looked awful. He looked tired and so sad that she had to swallow hard to keep her tears at bay. But seeing him also made her heart swell with her love for him and she was glad she had come, no matter the outcome.

She walked toward him and when she reached him, as afraid as she was by what his reaction might be, she met his gaze bravely.

He groaned. "My mother came to your house."

She nodded.

He closed his eyes for a moment and pressed his hand to his forehead. "I'm sorry. She told me she was going to her friend Trudy's. I should have known better."

"*Nay*, I'm glad she came. We need to talk, Elden, because I made a terrible mistake. I saw you and Mary together and she was flirting with you and you were smiling and..." Against her will, the tears came anyway. "And I thought you'd rather be with her than me."

"Millie—"

"*Nay*," she interrupted, clasping her hands together. "Let me finish before I lose my nerve."

"At least come into the barn. It's cold out here." He led her inside, leaving the doors open.

Millie watched her father throw a stick for Samson to fetch, then followed Elden inside. "I broke up with you because I had so little confidence in myself—" she shrugged "—in your love for me, that I thought that even if it wasn't Mary you would rather have, it would be some other girl. The next girl who flirted with you. It sounds silly even saying it out loud now, Elden, but I broke our betrothal so you couldn't."

"Why would I break up with you, Millie? I told you I loved you. I asked you to marry me." His brow creased beneath his knit cap as he tried to comprehend. "Why would you think even for a moment that I didn't want you?"

Her lower lip trembled. "I don't know. Because I'm fat and ugly and...*fat*," she repeated.

"Oh, Millie." He put his arms around her and held her tight. "I'm so sorry. I'm not good at this, at courting. This is my fault. I should have told you how beautiful you are every day. How smart and capable and so perfect for me."

Millie clung to him, breathing in deeply the male scent of him as her tears dampened his coat.

"This isn't your fault. It's mine." He leaned back to look into her eyes, but he didn't let go of her. "I knew this had to do with Mary. At least, indirectly. I should have followed you that day and made you talk to me. Every day since you broke up with me, I've told myself I should go to you, but I was scared."

"Of me? Why?" she breathed.

"Because...because I didn't think I was good enough for you, Millie. You're not the only one who struggles with self-confidence.

After Mary broke up with me, I believed no woman would want me. I rationalized that if I wasn't good enough for her, how could I be good enough for anyone. Then I fell in love with you and dreamed of a life with you, but I worried you'd break up with me, too. And when you did—" He took a deep breath and exhaled. "When you did, I thought—I don't know what I thought. That I was unlovable?"

"Oh, Elden. What a mess we've made of this." She laughed through her tears as she hugged him tightly. "I'm so sorry my insecurities made you feel insecure. I do love you. I love you so much." She gazed into his blue-gray eyes. "And I'll marry you, if you'll have me."

"*If* I'll have you?" He laughed. "I think all I've ever wanted is you, Millie. And I think that together we can work on this, on believing in ourselves. I know I can, just knowing you believe in me." He brushed a lock of blond hair that had escaped her headscarf. "I really want to kiss you right now. Can I kiss you?"

She nodded and closed her eyes. As his mouth touched hers for the very first time, she felt as if she was melting into his arms.

"This is why a father needs to escort his daughter," her father said, startling them both. Elden and Millie parted, both looking sheepish, and her father walked into the barn, the bulldog at his feet. "This mean we're having a wedding at my place?" he asked, looking from one to the other.

"Um…it does," Elden managed. "With your permission."

Her father smiled, lifting his shoulders with excitement. "A wedding. That's just what the Koffman family needs now." He looked upward. "Don't we, Aggie?" Then he turned to the open door. "Look! It's snowing!" He laughed like a child and rushed back outside, the dog at his heels.

"I think that was a yes," Elden said, meeting Millie's gaze again. He held out his hand and led her out of the barn and into the snow. "Merry Christmas, my love."

"Merry Christmas," she whispered, and then she rested her head on Elden's shoulder, knowing he would be her husband and that they would have as happy a marriage as she had ever dreamed of.

Epilogue

~~

Millie walked into the kitchen that smelled of evergreens she and Elden had cut fresh from their woods and of the cinnamon, cloves and orange peels that simmered on the back of the woodstove. Chilled, she went straight to the stove to warm her hands.

"There you are." Elden greeted her with a warm smile. He was putting away the last of the clean dishes from their Christmas Eve supper. Because they were spending all of Christmas Day with her family, they had decided to have a quiet night at home alone tonight.

"Here I am," she smiled back. Although they'd been married more than a year, she still couldn't believe this handsome man had chosen her above all the other unmarried women in Honeycomb. But she was so thankful every day that he had.

Elden carried his mother's blue onion serving platter to the dish cabinet. "How'd it go? Everything *oll recht*?"

She rubbed her hands together to warm them. She didn't know if they'd have snow for Christmas, but it was certainly bitterly cold outside. "*Oll goot*. She's tucked in for the night, a warm brick at her feet and hot water bottle under the quilts."

"No fussing?" he asked.

She grinned. "A bit, but you know how she is. I said Livie, it's bedtime." After they married, Millie hadn't been able to call Lavinia "Mother" as many married women called their mothers-in-law, so she had shortened Lavinia to Livie. Surprisingly, his mother liked Millie's pet name for her. "I said, 'You can stay up all night if you want, but we're going to bed.'" She shrugged. "I gave her the Bible and she seemed content. But she kept telling me to send you over to get her if we need her. She said she didn't care if it was the middle of the night. I told her we'd be just fine, you and I."

It had been Elden's idea to build a *grossmammi* house a short walk from the big house before he and Millie were married. Because they had chosen to wait a full year after they began courting to wed, he'd had the time to build the small one-story house for his mother. And thanks to his thoughtfulness, Millie, as a new bride, never had spent a single night under the same roof with her mother-in-law. "How are things here?"

Closing the dish cabinet door, he walked over to stand beside her in front of the stove, the scent of applewood filling the cozy kitchen to mingle with the other smells of Christmas. *"Goot."* He grinned, obviously proud of himself. "All tucked in and sound asleep last I checked."

"And David didn't give you any trouble? No fussing?" They both smiled at the little joke between them. Named after Elden's father, David was often fussy and there were times when Lavinia was able to soothe him when neither of them could. Elden believed that his son's nature was similar to his grandmother's, so the baby gravitated to her.

"No fussing," Elden confirmed. "David snuggled right in next to Aggie and they're both sound asleep. Thank you for walking *Mam* back to her house and getting her situated. By the time supper was over, I was close to being out of patience with her."

Millie gazed into his eyes, unable to stop

smiling. She didn't think she'd stopped grinning since the day they were wed. "You'd run out of patience for your mother, but you still had patience for two *bopplis* barely three months old?"

He shrugged. "Not much for me to do. You'd already fed, changed them and dressed them in their sleeping gowns. All Samson and I had to do was put them to bed. Easy enough. I rocked one and Samson rocked the other."

Millie laughed and poked her husband in the side. Since they'd married, he'd filled out a bit and become more muscular. All the good food Millie cooked for him, he said. "You're not supposed to rock them to sleep every night. They need to learn to settle on their own."

"You hear that, boy?" Elden said to Samson, who lay on a rag rug beside the stove. "She doesn't want us rocking our babies."

The bulldog cocked his head as if as perplexed as his master.

Millie laughed and wagged her finger. "The two of you best not come whining to me a year from now when the babies are still not sleeping through the night."

"Speaking of sleeping through the night." Elden glanced at the clock on the wall. "We best get to bed. They'll be awake in another three hours, wanting to be fed again."

"*Ach*, you're right." Millie turned to look at the kitchen. "What's left to be done before we go upstairs?"

"Not a thing." Elden took her by the hand and led her toward the staircase. As they walked out of the kitchen, he stopped to turn off the oil lamp.

A warm, velvety darkness settled around them and Millie moved closer to her husband. "*Danki*," she whispered.

His breath was warm on her cheek. "For what?"

"For everything," she said. "For this home… our babies and for—" Emotion rose in her throat, and it took her a moment to speak again. "For loving me, Elden."

He leaned closer, his voice deep and rich and gentle. "You make it so easy to love you, Millie. Thank you for loving me. For making me a better man than I was. For helping me believe I could be a man worthy of your love."

And then her husband kissed her, and she wished the moment would last until Christmas morning. And the Christmas morning after that and beyond.

* * * * *

Dear Reader,

I hope you enjoyed the first book in my new series featuring the Koffman family, *Seven Amish Sisters*. As I created the characters, I found myself wanting to join Millie and her sisters and their father at their supper table.

And isn't Millie a wonderful young woman? She and Elden struggled to make their way, but thankfully, in the end, with God's help, they found love. Like Millie and Elden, I think we all struggle with self-confidence at times and in those times, we need to look to those who love us, and to God to help us believe in ourselves.

If you enjoyed Millie and Elden's story, I hope you'll return to Honeycomb to see which sister will fall in love next. I have a feeling it might be Beth!

Blessings,
Emma Miller

Get 4 FREE REWARDS!

We'll send you 2 FREE Books plus 2 FREE Mystery Gifts.

FREE Value Over **$20**

Both the **Love Inspired®** and **Love Inspired® Suspense** series feature compelling novels filled with inspirational romance, faith, forgiveness, and hope.

Get 4 FREE REWARDS!

We'll send you 2 FREE Books plus 2 FREE Mystery Gifts.

FREE
Value Over
$20

Both the **Harlequin® Special Edition** and **Harlequin® Heartwarming™** series feature compelling novels filled with stories of love and strength where the bonds of friendship, family and community unite.

YES! Please send me 2 FREE novels from the Harlequin Special Edition or Harlequin Heartwarming series and my 2 FREE gifts (gifts are worth about $10 retail). After receiving them, if I don't wish to receive any more books, I can return the shipping statement marked "cancel." If I don't cancel, I will receive 6 brand-new Harlequin Special Edition books every month and be billed just $5.24 each in the U.S. or $5.99 each in Canada, a savings of at least 13% off the cover price or 4 brand-new Harlequin Heartwarming Larger-Print books every month and be billed just $5.99 each in the U.S. or $6.49 each in Canada, a savings of at least 20% off the cover price. It's quite a bargain! Shipping and handling is just 50¢ per book in the U.S. and $1.25 per book in Canada.* I understand that accepting the 2 free books and gifts places me under no obligation to buy anything. I can always return a shipment and cancel at any time by calling the number below. The free books and gifts are mine to keep no matter what I decide.

Choose one: ☐ **Harlequin Special Edition** ☐ **Harlequin Heartwarming**
(235/335 HDN GRCQ) **Larger-Print**
(161/361 HDN GRC3)

Name (please print)

Address   Apt. #

City   State/Province   Zip/Postal Code

Email: Please check this box ☐ if you would like to receive newsletters and promotional emails from Harlequin Enterprises ULC and its affiliates. You can unsubscribe anytime.

> ### Mail to the **Harlequin Reader Service:**
> **IN U.S.A.:** P.O. Box 1341, Buffalo, NY 14240-8531
> **IN CANADA:** P.O. Box 603, Fort Erie, Ontario L2A 5X3
>
> Want to try 2 free books from another series! Call 1-800-873-8635 or visit www.ReaderService.com.

*Terms and prices subject to change without notice. Prices do not include sales taxes, which will be charged (if applicable) based on your state or country of residence. Canadian residents will be charged applicable taxes. Offer not valid in Quebec. This offer is limited to one order per household. Books received may not be as shown. Not valid for current subscribers to the Harlequin Special Edition or Harlequin Heartwarming series. All orders subject to approval. Credit or debit balances in a customer's account(s) may be offset by any other outstanding balance owed by or to the customer. Please allow 4 to 6 weeks for delivery. Offer available while quantities last.

Your Privacy—Your information is being collected by Harlequin Enterprises ULC, operating as Harlequin Reader Service. For a complete summary of the information we collect, how we use this information and to whom it is disclosed, please visit our privacy notice located at corporate.harlequin.com/privacy-notice. From time to time we may also exchange your personal information with reputable third parties. If you wish to opt out of this sharing of your personal information, please visit readerservice.com/consumerschoice or call 1-800-873-8635. **Notice to California Residents**—Under California law, you have specific rights to control and access your data. For more information on these rights and how to exercise them, visit corporate.harlequin.com/california-privacy.

HSEHW22R2

COUNTRY LEGACY COLLECTION

19 FREE BOOKS IN ALL!

EMMETT
Diana Palmer

COURTED BY THE COWBOY
Sasha Summers

THE RANCHER AND THE BABY
Marie Ferrarella

Cowboys, adventure and romance await you in this new collection! Enjoy superb reading all year long with books by bestselling authors like Diana Palmer, Sasha Summers and Marie Ferrarella!

COMING NEXT MONTH FROM
Love Inspired

SNOWBOUND AMISH CHRISTMAS
Amish of Prince Edward Island • by Jo Ann Brown

Kirsten Petersheim's new life plan involves making a success of her housecleaning business—and doesn't include love. Then her new client Mark Yutzy asks for advice about dealing with his troubled teenage brother. This Christmas she might reconsider a future that involves the handsome farmer.

AN AMISH CHRISTMAS INHERITANCE
by Virginia Wise

When Katie Schwartz inherits her late aunt's farm in Lancaster County, she's eager to run her own business. But widowed single dad Levi Miller owns half the farm and isn't giving up without a fight. When they must unite to save the property from foreclosure, will they discover they share more than an inheritance?

THE MISTLETOE FAVOR
Wyoming Ranchers • by Jill Kemerer

With the holidays approaching, wealthy rancher and new guardian Mac Tolbert enlists coffee shop owner Bridget Renna to hire his withdrawn teenage sister. Fresh from New York, Bridget is doing her best to live independently in Wyoming, but as she bonds with Kaylee and soon Mac, will the truth about her past threaten their growing love?

HER SECRET SON
Sundown Valley • by Linda Goodnight

After discovering injured Nash Corbin on her ranch, Harlow Matheson is surprised at how quickly long-buried feelings begin to resurface. For Nash, spending time with the girl he left behind is the best part of this homecoming. Until he meets the son he never knew existed...

THE CHRISTMAS SWITCH
by Zoey Marie Jackson

Switching places with her twin sister wasn't part of Chanel Houston's holiday plans. Yet with a sibling in need, she can't refuse to help. But as she falls for her sister's next-door neighbor Ryder Frost, his adorable little girl and his rowdy puppy, can she keep the secret?

A NANNY FOR THE RANCHER'S TWINS
by Heidi Main

Cattle rancher Ethan McCaw desperately needs a nanny for his twin daughters. His neighbor Laney Taylor is seeking a contractor to convert her house into a wedding venue. He'll agree to renovate her place if she cares for his girls. Can they take a chance on a future—together?

LOOK FOR THESE AND OTHER LOVE INSPIRED BOOKS WHEREVER BOOKS ARE SOLD, INCLUDING MOST BOOKSTORES, SUPERMARKETS, DISCOUNT STORES AND DRUGSTORES.

LICNM0922